I0626128

THE
WRACK
LINE

NOT THE WHITTAKER PRIZE 2013

© 2014 THE RIGHTEYEDDEER PRESS

Edited by John Wilks
on behalf of The Write Idea

Poems and short stories © individual authors.

The authors credited for the material contained in this anthology
assert their moral rights to be identified as the author
of that material.

This material cannot be reproduced without permission.

contact: Donna Gagnon & Douglas Pugh
TheRightEyedDeer Press
PO Box 236
Haliburton, ON
Canada K0M 1S0

http://therighteyeddeer.weebly.com

ISBN 978-0-9921679-1-2

FOREWORD:

Foreword	*John Wilks*	7
Agree A Separation	*Mandy Pannett*	9
Heron	*Jeff Pinkney*	10
His Daughter's Voice	*Rachel Green*	11
Spotted Touch-Me-Not	*F.H. Lee*	16
Pigeons And Gulls	*Rhonda Parrish*	18
Do You Believe In Unicorns...?	*Anne Hamlett*	21
Nevertime	*Colin Rennie*	22
Whispering Answers	*Bob Smith*	23
Taking A Break	*E.Russell Smith*	28
Always In Your Heart	*Vicky Daddo*	29
No More Lullabies	*Effie Merryl*	33
Blue Widow	*Eilidh Thomas*	35
patience	*Francis Hayes*	36
Family Gatherings	*Douglas Pugh*	37
After School	*Joss Hayes*	43
Recycled Lives	*Eilidh Thomas*	44
October	*Francis Hayes*	48
Dark Dissonance	*Douglas Pugh*	51
Common Ground	*Gill Terry*	52
A Problem With Dogs	*Joss Hayes*	53
Easy	*F.H. Lee*	56
Per Ardua Ad Astra	*Gill Terry*	57
Hands On Approach	*Effie Merryl*	61
Yue Yue	*Jeff Pinkney*	66
Hazel	*Anne Hamlett*	67
An Angel To The Rescue	*Bob Smith*	68
Radio 2 FM	*E.Russell Smith*	73
Bad Riddance	*Rachel Green*	74
Sparrow	*Colin Rennie*	79
The Wrack Line	*Mandy Pannett*	80
Contributors		82

The line of dried seaweed, marine vegetation, and other organic debris and detritus left on the beach by the action of the tides is called the wrack line.

Between September and December 2013, the tides of creativity threw much flotsam and jetsam onto the shores of The Write Idea. Sixty-three stories and one hundred poems emerged from the ocean depths of imagination and basked beneath the unforgiving light of twenty-five pairs of judgmental eyes.

This compilation is fashioned from thirty pieces of driftwood garnered from those beached ideas...

Oh, how we writers love our extended metaphors.

NOT The Whittaker Prize 2013 was two competitions of six rounds each, running on alternate weeks. Six weeks of short fiction and six weeks of poetry. Each round, five prompts were provided for inspiration purposes: music, quotes, artwork, historical events and videos. Entrants had two weeks in which to compose their entries, then a further two weeks in which to score the work of their competitors. The winners were determined by the total aggregate scores at the end of round six.

Some scores were generous. Others tough. Brutal, even. And no two entrants agreed with each other. One person's 9-point 'I wish I'd written that' was another person's 3-point 'back to the drawing board'.

Even so, three clear winners emerged:

Fiction: **Jon Pinnock**

Poetry: **Mandy Pannett**

Combined fiction & poetry: **Gill Terry**

Congratulations to them and to all who took part. The nature of this competition relied on everyone staying the course and playing fair. It was a pleasure (and honour) to administer.

I trust you will continue to write and send your messages in bottles so long as the tides persist in turning.

MANDY PANNETT

and we could watch the city sparrows
pecking around this station bar
blown in by the windy platform's
draught from a leaving train

and we'd discuss why Russian starlings
seek out the cold of our southern shores
or recall a night in the Welney Fens
where rivers were silver under the moon
and the wetlands wild with geese

we might remember the seagull
who mistook our bedroom window for sky
and how the smear of its small face
stayed on the glass for hours

and we'd agree a separation
would be painful too
and wonder if the bird survived
to lift its wings and fly again though
bruised – we hope it tried we'd say
we hope it really tried

HERON

JEFF PINKNEY

Heron offers no goodbyes,
nor cares what fate
has named the river.
Heron speaks in arrows,
but will not point the way.

Heron sees in you the child,
and has flown above your grave.

Because heron has no lies
there's no need to fish for truth.
And heron knows that time—
when flowing backwards,
is just another shade of blue.

His Daughter's Voice

RACHEL GREEN

It was like meditation, sitting alone in the park on a cold October afternoon. The wind on the water, the weak sunshine barely warming the air, the sound of the ducks doing whatever it was ducks did. The wind sent leaves eddying around the bench, a tiny funnel of dry crackling in the gold of his daughter's hair. It was odd that he only ever thought of Becky. Margaret never popped into his thoughts, except to make him feel guilty for not thinking about her. He would have expected to miss his wife more than his child since they'd spent long, intimate years together but that was never the case. Perhaps this was less a meditation than a penance.

Gerald looked down at his sketch. What should have been the boating lake surrounded by scantily clad acers and willows had become another portrait of his long-lost daughter. That was when he heard the music. It was pop music – rubbish, really, but his dad had thought the same when he listened to rock and roll – but he was sure he recognised it. Certain, really. He could picture the singer, a tall woman with close-cropped red hair and obscenely red lips, Disgusting lyrics about sex and abuse, though he could never work out if it was about a man abusing a woman or the other way round. Becky had loved it, of course, as teenagers were wont to do. He would have banned it from the house but it would only have made her love it more. Better to grin and bear it and wait for her to tire of the song.

Now here it was again, playing at the very spot where she'd died, all those years ago. It was a sign, surely? Not that he believed in such things but he'd get down on his knees and pray if it meant he got his sweet daughter back again, even if only for a minute.

He pushed himself to his feet and crossed the path to the edge of the lake. He was right. This was Becky's song, drifting faintly over the water. Was she down there? "Becky?" He fell to his knees. "Becky, my darling. Come to Daddy."

He clasped his hands together in prayer to a God he hadn't believed in for thirty years. "Let her come to me, just for a minute. Just for the length of the song. I've never asked for anything else, have I? I'll come to church every day. I'll give everything I have to charity. I'll enrol in the clergy. Just let me see my Becky again, just for a minute."

He stared out over the water but there was nothing. Just the sunlight glinting off the ripples and the sound of a crow calling from one of the sycamores around the edge of the lake and a woman walking the perimeter. She changed course when she saw him and as she got closer he realised it was a girl rather than a grown woman, a chubby teenager with unnaturally orange hair cropped, at a guess, with the aid of a mirror and a pair of nail scissors. One ear was plugged by an earbud connected to a mobile phone, the earbud's twin dangled over her stomach.

"You all right, Granddad?" She looked nothing like his Becky. "You praying for inspiration or have you lost a contact lens?"

"No, I..." Embarrassed, Gerald tried to think of a reason for being on his knees in the damp earth. "I fell. An old wound." He struggled to his feet, tapping his leg to add credence to the lie. "Shouldn't you be in school?"

"Personal day." She slipped her rucksack off her shoulders and sat on the other end of the bench, then proceeded to open the bag and extract a packet of crisps.

Gerald fumed silently. Why did she have to sit on his bench? This had been his bench for thirty years, ever since the accident. There was even a little brass plaque fixed to it. Presented to Laverstone Borough Council by Gerald Turner in memory of his daughter Rebecca. Not that anybody ever read it. He picked up his sketchbook and pencil again, though his mind was no longer on sketching. Not with somebody watching.

He glanced along the bench. The girl was digging into a packet of crisps, feeding them into her mouth one after another without even waiting for her mouth to empty in between. It was no wonder she was the size of a small house. Still, she looked after her hair, albeit with a shade of copper that was as natural as a plastic palm tree. She finished the crisps by upending the crumbs into her mouth, then smoothed out the packet, folding it over and over into a tiny triangle. After a few moments she reached into the bag at her feet and withdrew a second pack. He gave her a smile. "What's a pretty girl like you doing out here on your own?"

She didn't answer, just stared fixedly ahead. He could see the headphones in her ears, though he couldn't hear any music. He reached across and tapped her on the arm. She jumped, sending bacon flavour crisps over the ground. "What?"

"Are you waiting for someone?"

"None of your business."

"I only ask because it seems off, you sitting here all on your own."

"You're on your own as well."

He grimaces, raising his hands outward. "I'm an old man. All I've got is alone."

"Me too." She looked into her crisp packet, turned the open top towards him. "You want a crisp?"

Gerald hesitated. Crisps got under his dental plate, but to refuse would seem churlish. He reached into the packet. "Thank you."

"S'alright." She watched him transfer the crisp to his mouth before taking another for herself. "What're you doin'?"

He looked down at his book where Becky gazed out with her perpetual half-smile. What he wouldn't give to see her again. She would have known how to respond to this child. Everybody loved

Becky. That was what was so beautiful about her. She'd have become instant friends with this girl. Better than him, anyway. He turned the book to show her. "It's my daughter."

"Drawing? That's pretty good." The girl looked around. "Who's she then? Your wife?"

"My daughter. She died a long time ago." He shook his head to clear it of the past. "What are you listening to? Anything I know?"

"Maybe." She pulled one earplug out and held it out to him. "Here."

He looked at it and swallowed. She'd just pulled it out of her ear. What if it had her wax on it? He compromised, bending his head over the yellow plastic without actually touching it. "All I can hear is static."

"Yeah." She screwed the plug back into her ear. "Sometimes you can hear voices in it."

"Voices?"

"Ghosts."

Gerald gave a short bark of laughter, suddenly afraid this strange girl was even stranger than she appeared. Was she a psych patient on day release? Was she dangerous? "I'm not sure what you mean."

"I've heard ghosts can communicate through white noise. The theory is, if there's an unmodulated sound present, it's easier to affect that noise than make a new one from scratch. Supposedly it takes a lot of energy for a ghost to actually speak but much less for one to alter an electrical field."

"That makes a sort of sense." Not that he believed in ghosts. If he did, he'd have spent the last thirty years either trying to contact Becky or else trying to lay her soul to rest. Assuming her death was violent, which he'd never know. He'd heard at the time that drowning was a peaceful way to go. He couldn't remember who'd told him that. Someone who'd looked after the body. A coroner or undertaker. They'd know if anyone did. He pursed his lips. "So... Have you heard any?"

"Maybe." She looked out over the lake as is debating whether to elaborate. "Sometimes I just hear radio stations on the very edge of tuning. Have you ever used a short-wave radio?"

"Yes, of course." Her question brought a recollection of his grandfather's radiogram, a monstrosity the size of a large sideboard which took upwards of ten minutes to warm up, the valves inside glowing orange. He remembered long evenings when he was on holiday there, turning the dial from longwave to shortwave, listening in on snatches of broadcasts in foreign languages amid the whistles and hisses of static.

"It sounds like that. Snatches of conversation on the very edge of audibility and then a few moments later it's gone again." She grinned suddenly. "Sometimes I get nothing at all. It's dead boring."

"They say ghosts are echoes of our future selves, glimpses between the cracks of time and space."

"Give over. You're going to tell me you live in a telephone box in a minute."

"Like Doctor Who?" He laughed. "I don't think so. I wish I was. I could do with a regeneration into a younger body." He turned away from her again, looking out over the lake. That's where they'd found Becky. Right there, by that overhanging willow, only it was a sapling then. No taller than him and ramrod straight. Now it was taller than most houses and with a pronounced list, great ropes of root anchoring it to the ground and the lake bed. When he turned back he realised she was crying. "Are you all right?"

She wiped her face, as if embarrassed by the tears. "My brother died."

If he was taken aback by the sudden shift in conversation he tried not to show it. "Oh! How terribly sad. I'm so sorry. Was he older or younger than you?"

"Younger. It was an accident."

"How tragic. What was his name? What happened?"

"Dean. He got run over. Mum and Dad kind of drifted apart after that."

"What about you? How did you feel about it?"

"Really sad, obviously. He was my brother, after all. What was really weird was the way everything carried on so mechanically. Mum and Dad were like robots, you know? Get up. Go to work. Come home. Eat. Sleep. Rinse and repeat. I couldn't see the point. It didn't seem to matter if I went to school or not. I doubt they even noticed if I was in the house or not."

"I'm sure that's not true at all."

"It is, though. They didn't give a shit about me. Even before he died Dean was always the golden boy. He was in the bottom set for everything and it didn't matter. If I wasn't top of every class I used to get a bollocking."

She sniffed, and the sound made Gerald look up in surprise. Her tone of voice had been so perfectly level he hadn't even noticed how upset she was. The clinical outlook was a crumbling façade and he could see glimpses of the frightened, lonely little girl underneath. "So they didn't talk to you about Dean?"

"No. Not a word. It was as if he ceased to exist the moment he was buried and we all had to deal with the missing piece of our lives without seeing if they fitted to anyone else's."

"That must have been very difficult for you." Gerald was pleased with himself. Why couldn't he have talked to Becky like this after Mary died? Because Becky blamed him for her death, a still, small voice replied.

"You think?" The girl glared at him for a moment, then her features softened. "We all dealt with it in our own ways. That was the problem." She pulled a chocolate bar from her jacket and began to unwrap it. He recognised the distinctive logo of a KitKat. "What happened to your daughter?"

"She drowned." Gerald pointed to the lake. "Right there, actually."

She'd just taken a bite across all four chocolate fingers but her mouth had fallen open. She spoke with her mouth full. "Becky. That's short for Rebecca, ennit?"

"That's right. We named her after her grandmother."

She stood, stuffing the rest of the KitKat in her mouth and balling up the wrapper. "I've got to go." Hoisting the rucksack over one shoulder and putting one of the earbuds in, she fiddled with the menu. He heard a growling, masculine voice: "Sweet dreams are made of this..." That explained his miraculous memory jog earlier. She began to walk away, then turned. "Here, mate?"

"Yes?"

"Have a gander on me." The young girl lifted her jumper, the cotton tee shirt beneath riding up to reveal an expanse of pale flesh wider than his wife's when she was about to give birth. The fabric caught on the underside of her expansive breasts, tautening under the strain then popping up like air trapped in a U-bend to reveal the pale twin moons of her cleavage in their underwired bra. Gerald wanted to look away but couldn't, staring open-mouthed at the scene but unable to voice the words to stop it.

The moment passed and she lowered her woollen curtain over the gate of Earthly Delight. "Somethin' to keep you going, yeah? Something to get you hard when they put you in your bath tub at the nursing home."

He wanted to tell her he wasn't in a nursing home. He wanted to tell her he had a house not ten minutes walk away. He wanted to tell her not to flash her tits at strange old men it the park.

Most of all, he wanted to tell her she was beautiful.

F H LEE

(impatiens capensis)

Widow Stanley gripped the pew curlicue with her gnarled hand
to steady a creaky genuflection. A patchwork quilt of liverspots
coloured tissue-thin skin hidden beneath snug black gloves.

A rarity, this Jewelweed, to arrive early for her precious time
near the stained glass window she had favoured for 24 years,
to contemplate this and many other advents, celebrate the wait.

Colours no longer worn on cloth or cheek; pale blue with light
shades of lavender, a mantle of splendor. In the scene, Eve
dreams beneath the apple tree, feeds a partridge in the grass.

Adam sees Eve, not the serpent with an apple lodged in its fangs,
with a gleam in one yellow eye fixed on the fated couple. Adam
sees no black, no night, only the glow from his one and only lady.

She will mother two sons, be honoured and blamed and remain
undefined for all time, cloaked in suspicion, pain, hostility. Adam
will share the grief of losing one son by the hand of the other.

The widow named the bird Clem, after her late husband. She too
gave up gardening, unwilling to part with the peace of it all. The
bird had taken its name when she'd returned to this earlier view.

The glass bird with blue plumage had been a "pet" since childhood, when
she'd fainted at age twelve, ten minutes into her very first Midnight Mass.
Ancient radiator pipes hissed out heat, stealing breath from her pale lips.

Her father would not allow her to leave, but filled her lungs with fresh
crisp night air, used snow to stop the bleeding, ease swelling. Told her
to focus on something lovely; red, green, gold votive candles. Song.

With her head against the small soft shoulder of her mother's coat,
her eyes first spotted Clem, tawny and tufted. Her initial thought was
why an apple tree and not a pear? But he was there, all year long.

Her crooked knuckle brushed against that old scar of initiation, as
the other hand dropped her widow's mite into the collection basket
carefully held by a newborn babe fresh out his straw-lined manger.

Advent. The season of waiting. Widow Stanley had prepared well for this day, to meet her maker. Her impatience to see the garden saddened her son. All that penance and prayer. A long life wasted.

The walk back to her house of straw was unremarkable. Her son tried to upgrade it to at least sticks, if not bricks. She refused. Stayed closer to humble goals, to Clem, to Eve. Each novena forged an invisible brick.

The shadow outside the house could not cross her threshold, as a single light pulsed within. It dissolved into an empty snakeskin of ash on the sidewalk. No point returning. She had earned her peaceful death.

He could tell from the instant he stepped out of the airport that he was in a different country. It smelled different. Saltier, wetter. There was no doubt that it was an island, and about as far removed from his rural Saskatchewan upbringing as it was possible to be. Intimidating, to be sure, but it was excitement which coiled in his belly as he boarded the bus which would take him to his new life. Excitement, not fear.

They were meant to be. That's what they'd told each other in the millions of instant messages they'd exchanged, the thousands of emails, hundreds of phone calls. Meant to be. No question. Two parts of the same whole; soulmates. It only made sense that he would come to live with her, his life was portable, hers was not, and there was also the question of her daughter, Emily.

He couldn't ask her to uproot her daughter, the little girl who owned as big a piece of his heart as her mother did. The darling who'd begun calling him 'Daddy' on his first visit six months ago. He couldn't ask Emily, barely three, to give up everyone and everything she knew to come to a different country, a different life.

And what was he leaving anyway?

He'd never really fit in his hometown. Its people were too narrow-minded to accept him. His style was far too confrontational, his ideas too liberal, his voice too loud. He had survived years and years of bullying, by children and adults alike, because he didn't fit within their mold, he would not miss them once he was gone. And besides, it was an adventure. A new country, a new family, a new life.

Things started well, their little family of three. His girlfriend would go to work each day and he would stay home with their daughter. He'd work from the computer, same as he had on the other side of the ocean, though it always required me to stop and think before picking up the phone or sending an email to a co-worker -- time zones were a bitch. Still, it was nicer, warmer, to be spending his days with Emily providing the background noise instead of his old radio. Was dream-like to take her out to the park to enjoy their lunch as a picnic, to feel her fingers curl around his as they strode down the street with cars rushing by (on the wrong side of the road).

Then what had felt like a perfect fit began to pinch in ways he'd never have expected.

He missed the sky. His girlfriend, Stephanie, looked at him like he was crazy when he said that, the pointed meaningfully up at the patch of blue above their heads. She didn't get it, he said, she couldn't get it. This is where she'd grown up, the only country she'd ever been to. To her it was normal to have to look upwards to see the sky, to him it was claustrophobic. He'd been raised in the middle of the prairies, where no matter where you looked you could see sky and open space. Even in the cities... at least, much more than here.

Here, he tried to explain, he felt like all the buildings were leaning in toward him, menacing him, blocking out the sky.

Didn't she ever want to see a horizon? A real horizon that wasn't interrupted by anything made by man? Where you could see where earth and sky met, not sky and steel, but sky and stone. Sky and dirt.

She didn't. She was offended on her country's behalf.

He was sorry.

He was sorry, but he didn't retract his words. Couldn't retract his words.

He started to miss people. People he never would have expected. Just random people he used to know. The regulars at the restaurant he'd cooked at, the woman who ran the corner store down the street, the pizza place that knew his order just from his name on their call display. He missed the touchstones of his old life. He'd expected to need to make changes, and for those changes to be challenging, but it wasn't the biggest things that plagued him, but the small. He couldn't find Minute Rice no matter how many shops he checked, and the temperatures on his oven were all in metric rather than imperial. Television shows were different, and you had to pay to have even the basic channels, and even local phone calls weren't free.

The highlight of his week began to be their Sunday trip to the market. They'd window shop and then head into McDonalds to pick up their lunch (even McDonalds was different, featuring banana milkshakes which they never did back home), and they'd take it to a churchyard, the building older than his entire country, to eat. But they wouldn't eat their fries. No, they saved those. Saved them and took them to the square where Emily would toss them into the clouds of pigeons and giggle wildly as they scattered then descended once more to feast on them.

She would run, arms outstretched and hair streaming, through the flock, laughing and screaming, while the birds took flight around her, drowning out her delighted sounds with the flapping of their wings, the cooing from their throats.

He'd stand with Stephanie and watch Emily. Watch with a smile stretched so far across his face that it hurt his cheeks, watch, smile and dream of expanding that moment, that feeling, to fill their entire lives and all the hours of their days.

But he couldn't do the impossible.

Stress and strain, homesickness and struggles began to wear, and eventually, one day, he and Stephanie both said words they couldn't take back. Hearts were broken, tears were cried, bags were packed, and before he had time to process what he was doing, he was on a plane back to the other side of the sea.

They tried to stay friendly, so he could remain part of Emily's life, but distance and time worked their destruction until all he had left were the memories of their times together, memories of the pigeons and the McDonald's french fries...

Coming back to the present he looked down at his hands, the familiar red box with the golden arches splashed across it. Peered down at the gulls that crowded around him on the sun-baked asphalt of the shopping mall parking lot and sighed. The birds' rude shrieks and greedy cries were nothing like the gentle coos and flutterings of the pigeons he missed so greatly.

He poured the box of fries out on the ground and then walked away. He didn't look back at the birds which gulped down his offering, but up at the sky that even here, in the heart of the city, was open, wide, visible.

Do You Believe In Unicorns...?

ANNE HAMLETT

My sister did, though she was born
with special gifts. It was the pink
plastic pony from Aunty Pat
which started her collection.

Then she saw an image in a book;
turned her ponies into unicorns
by making horns with plasticine
to stick on their heads.

Later, she said she'd seen real ones.
They'd come at night to comfort
her when upset, they were friends
who took her to magical places.

She'd describe their bright colours,
pearly pink, plush purple, sea green,
or ice blue. Special ones were crystal
white with long golden horns.

She'd see them slide down moonbeams
on starry nights, prance from mist
on rainy days or in the lane as we strolled
on walks – though we never saw them.

She grew older, lost her sense of time;
her reality was different to mine.
Now she's passed to a place
where unicorns belong.

Although yesterday -
I could have sworn I saw a unicorn
shimmer from a moonbeam,
with little Sis astride its back.

COLIN RENNIE

Ripped my skin off,
The wind did.
Or maybe it was the storm
Of your eyes
That peeled my layers away,
Lifted my lid
To peer underneath,
As if I'm hiding something.
But we both know nothing's there,
Only
Pipes, rusting nails, grit and steam,
Monoxide, dying cells and memories,
The millipede march of destiny
Struggling through veins and arteries,
But one day it will all be still,
When loneliness wraps me like a skin.

BOB SMITH

Clara Watson stared out her office window overlooking the cheese factory floor and thought, *I wish people were as easy to understand as cows.* It was only her fourth week on the job as manager at the new building, but already the pressure from head office was intense.

"Get that production up," Mr. Abbot had ranted. "We didn't invest all that money in a new state-of-the-art facility to see numbers what they were in the old one."

Just then, the phone rang, interrupting her contemplation.

"Ready, C.W.?" asked her husband. He was manager of the dairy production operation, and was facing his own challenge. Greenvalley Foods had bought up many of the surrounding farms, including theirs, which indirectly explained why she was sitting there. She and Charlie had realized they wouldn't be able to compete with the gigantic agri-business, especially now that they were in their fifties with no children to help out. So when Charlie negotiated the sale of their farm to them, he included him being manager of their dairy operation. After a few months to demonstrate his competence, he was in a position to recommend her for their new cheese operation when the former manager retired. Greenvalley had torn the ancient plant down and he had decided retirement was preferable to learning how to operate a modernized place.

"You kept the books and all the business things associated with running the farm," Charlie explained. "It can't be that much harder." It wasn't, except there had only been her and Charlie before, not other people to motivate and supervise.

However, he was now facing his own production crisis. Things had been fine over the summer when the cows had spent their days outside, but once the outdoor season was finished, that changed.

Now as she walked over to the multimillion dollar hi-tech barn Greenvalley had built beside the old cheese factory when their land acquisitions were complete, Clara remembered the tour Charlie had given her its first week. The place included a special room Charlie said was called a milking parlour. "It's so clean," he bragged, "even my mother would have approved." Clara knew that was high praise indeed. She recalled the plastic coverings on the furniture in the front room of the old Watson home, a place only used Christmas Day. Even then the smell of plastic had been obvious as it battled with pine.

"Check this out," Charlie had said, pointing to the speakers hanging in the corners of the barn. "Apparently cows like music, and happy cows give more milk."

Then he asked, "Smell that?" Clara couldn't smell anything, other than the subtle aroma of warm cattle that brought back girlhood memories of herding them in from the field, overlain by a faint waft of the newly-mown hay that now filled the upper floor.

"What am I supposed to be smelling?" she inquired.

"Exactly. In our old barn, the stench of manure was a constant, but not here. See that cable running down the middle of the floor?" Clara had barely noticed it, assumed it had something to do with the automatic feeding system Charlie raved about. "There are wide scrapers which extend across the entire floor that slowly travel down the length of the barn. Everything they pick up falls into the channel at the far end. It has a conveyer that takes everything outside to the manure pile. Not much smell and no work. I just have to hose down the place once a week," he said.

"What about the stalls?" she asked, looking around and for the first time noticing there weren't any.

"None. Cows just wander. That's where they get fed," he added, pointing to a contraption on the near-end wall. "It's computerized. Each cow has an individualized tag the sensor reads so the mechanism then delivers a mixture and portion size that's exactly right. No more guessing how much hay or grain to give them."

Her recollections ended as she reached the barn. "C.W.," he said as she entered. "Thanks for taking the time." She didn't tell him she welcomed any excuse to escape her own production quandary, which she knew had to be related to people since the facility itself and equipment were completely new.

"I want you to look around to see if you see anything," he continued. "I've adjusted their feed, had the veterinarian in to make sure there's no disease, even changed the music. Still no difference. I expected a minor reduction in milk when they came off fresh grass, but this is ridiculous. See if you can see anything."

Consulting her was not strange. On the farm, he had come to rely on her ability to recognize problems related to cows when he couldn't identify anything himself. Everyone assumed C.W. referred to her initials, and she didn't correct them. Actually, C.W. was his special nickname for her, short for Cow Whisperer. He had teasingly started calling her that after they went to see the movie The Horse Whisperer back in the '90's, a movie about a man with an uncanny ability to read horses. She had been enthusiastic about the movie, not because she loved riding as Charlie assumed, but because it starred Robert Redford. She found the sparkling blue eyes and dimpled chin in his rugged, chiselled visage more than compelling. However, she didn't tell Charlie that. The endearment C.W. was acceptable, maybe not romantic, but far better than the impersonal 'The Wife' or condescending 'Little Woman' she often heard other men use.

Once in Dairy Cattleman Monthly she had read an article that said cows thought in pictures, not words like people. She had always been more visual than others. In secondary school, Art was her favourite subject and Mr. Landry said she had talent and real potential. *Bet he didn't think I would end up using that ability on animals,* she thought. When Charlie hadn't been able to get one normally-placid cow into her stall at milking time one evening, Clara realized it was afraid of the rope Charlie had slung carelessly over the side wall. Another time, she had realized evening milking was much more challenging than morning milking, but only on sunny days. The sun reflected off the windshield of the old Ford beside the main door Charlie claimed he would get around to restoring someday, making a shimmering patch of brightness that spooked the cows. Under her tutelage, he had learned not to hang old towels on the pipes, and on windy days, to watch for blowing pieces of paper.

"I'll leave you to it," he said, hauling her back to the present. He knew she would meander through the barn, looking for anything unusual.

Twenty minutes later she called him. "That's the boss cow," she said, pointing to a big Holstein with a marking like a map of England on one side. "Whenever another cow goes to the feeding station, she nudges it away. Like all big cows, she can't run, so they get some food before she gets there, but they never finish and she eats the rest. That explains why your milk production is lower." She pointed to the other end. "Put in another feeding station down there. She can't guard them both."

Charlie nodded, indicating agreement.

On the way back through the parking lot, her mind once again turned to her own production problem. *I would love to have someone come in to the plant and solve things that easily,* she thought. *If only C.W. meant Citizen Whisperer or something.*

Thinking about how she had solved Charlie's problem, she decided to spend some time simply watching. Her office was at one end of the plant, above the refrigeration area, which was next to the production side with its tanks and vats. Outside the office, there was a wide catwalk behind a protective barrier, stairs at one end leading down to the plant floor. After she got back, she moved a chair out of the office, knowing her head would be the only thing visible above the railing.

At first, everything appeared to be normal. Raw milk was scalded, starter added, the curd was separated from the whey, and so on. Then Bessie Flaherty left her place at the end of the line hauling the heavy rounds of cheese to the refrigerator and marched over to Sally Bennet, busily operating the press which squeezed out whey that hadn't simply drained off. It was too noisy to hear what Bessie said but Sally slowed down, shaking her head and scowling after Bessie left. A few minutes later, Clara watched Bessie do the same with Mike Gagner by the Pasteurizing tank. Twice more in the next several minutes she watched Bessie approach someone, always with the same result, a shaking head and furrowed forehead, but a noticeable decrease in effort.

When Bessie had gone to Sally, Clara's reaction had been, *Bessie has too much time on her hands if she can leave her job like that.* She had assumed it would be a personal conversation. When it happened again with others, she knew it hadn't been but was mystified.

She went into her office and thought of what she knew about Bessie. She had only been there a few weeks, a new hire necessitated by the expansion. Clara had heard enough sexist comments over the years about how some jobs were 'men's jobs' because they required strength. *I would like to see them throwing hay bales or forcing a reluctant cow into a stall,* she had thought more than once. Therefore, she refused to consider gender when she hired, simply making certain the applicant had the necessary physique for the more demanding jobs. *Like hauling heavy cheese rounds,* she thought, picturing Bessie's arms. She had been impressed during the job interview when Bessie had said she had once had Olympic weight-lifting aspirations.

Clara thought of who in the plant might give her some straight answers. Grabbing the microphone for the address system, she called, "Jeanette Simons, please come to the office." Jeanette was a holdover, someone from the old plant who Clara had known for many years.

Clara grabbed a folder of papers which some day needed to go to the barn. When Jeanette arrived, she said, "I want to ask you about Bessie but I know you need an explanation for my call. When you go out, take this folder over to Charlie and tell people I forgot it just now and couldn't wait for this evening. That's your excuse. Actually, I want to know what's going on with Bessie."

Jeanette looked uncomfortable. After a brief silence, she said, "She wants to organize a union, with her as head. She makes everyone slow down. We don't really want to, but she's pretty intimidating." After a pause, she finished, "I need to leave right now. She won't believe me if I'm here long."

After Jeanette left, Clara leaned back in her chair. Her first thought was to fire Bessie, not for trying to organize a union but for intimidating people. *Can't do that,* she realized. *I don't think a union will make any difference since we already pay well and this place has modern safety features, but that's their choice. I can't seem like I'm interfering.* She twisted a lock of her greying hair around a finger, a sure sign she was thinking hard.

Grabbing the microphone again, she called, "Bessie, a minute?"

When Bessie arrived, she stood belligerently in front of Clara's desk, arms crossed. "Have a seat," Clara invited, trying to relax the woman. "There's an opportunity I want to discuss with you. It would mean more money come payday. I get tired of hearing men talk about women like we're all weaklings, and you're stronger than all of the others here." She figured a little flattery couldn't hurt. "Management intends to buy another delivery truck and they assume I will hire a man since the big cheese rounds are heavy and unloading will be part of the job. I've watched you moving them here and I know you could handle it. Not only that, you're local and know your way to all the small towns around here. The actual purchase is a few weeks away but

I don't want to wait until they tell me to hire a man, then start arguing. But first, I need to find out if you're interested. It would take you out of here all day, but I think you would work well independently. "

At least she uncrossed her arms, Clara thought. *And her expression changed to curiosity. This solution is not as simple as a second feeding station, but we're talking people, not cows. At least it gets her out of a position where she can nudge others.* Picturing the Holstein's efforts to prove she was top dog, Clara realized. Maybe people aren't so different after all, just a little more subtle. The Whisperer strikes again.

Taking A Break

E Russell Smith

We leave our north-east home
to its vicissitudes of weather, politics,
dollar signs and obligation, for these
south-western mornings, waking mild
and walking blue, where local ferments
can be someone else's business.

Thrown back upon our under-used
imaginations, day after glorious idle day,
we seek out challenges — standing up to
rolling waves, hang-gliding into canyons,
kiting over high hot chaparral, and dining
on black pudding, souse and sauerkraut.

Oleanders charm, but they are toxic;
camellias shed their blooms too soon.
Tropic fruits are soft and succulent —
we hanker for the snap of frost,
for lilac banks by greening fields,
crisp apples, McIntosh or Idared,

and at least three parties to our politics.
One disposes, one opposes, and the third
is left to give the others fresh ideas.
So they are allowed to carry on —
we keep the peace and study order;
we make sauerkraut, poetry and love.

VICKY DADDO

She hadn't set foot in the place for years. It was easy to stay away when you put your mind to it. Besides, it was a long drive these days. In the early days, when grief was a cruel and scratching thing that clawed at her insides, she bargained with God. She promised him she would pray if he didn't make her visit the graveyard. She told Him she didn't need a headstone to weep at or to lay flowers in person. What she didn't tell Him was that she had done all the praying before. She didn't tell Him that praying didn't work. Nothing worked. It had been futile. Futile. She'd looked it up once. Useless, ineffectual, vain. Frivolous, trifling. It was how life was now. And that was as it should be.

But now the storm of the decade had passed over the churchyard she knew she had to go. It was like the wind had pulled her.

The grave was in the newer section of the yard, past the ornate Italian section with the grandiose marble headstones, past the Greek section with its vaguely unsettling photos of the deceased embossed in the uprights of their miniature Parthenons, past the Dutch section with the creaky windmills and simple epitaphs. The old section with mossy headstones on the lean and indecipherable words etched with muck and grime was usually shadowed by thick-limbed Blackwoods but the pair had been uprooted leaving gum bark and limbs scattered around. A small selection of gravestones had borne the brunt of the trees' branches and were broken or pushed over into the soft earth. Madeleine feared she would see bones poking through the mud. Her skin crawled with goosebumps as she hunkered down and battled past.

When she arrived at the grave the ground was strewn with gum bark, leaves shivering in puddles that pooled against the headstones, flowers – artificial and real – were broken and shrivelled in clumps against the trunks of trees. There were small branches lodged at all angles in the ground or across graves. People were busy with wheelbarrows, rakes and brooms. They were busy. They were doing. They were helping. Madeleine watched with a mixture of envy and relief.

"Bad storm," one of them said, stopping his wheelbarrow next to the grave. "Terrible mess but we'll have it cleaned up in no time. Can't have all these poor souls covered in muck." He moved a gloved hand around.

Poor souls. She shivered but didn't reply.

At last someone delivered a hamper of food and keep cups filled with hot drinks. The workers left their tools and took shelter from the threatening skies in the small chapel. Madeleine pulled her beanie down over her ears and snuggled her hands deep into the pockets of her coat. She kicked a clump of sodden leaves away from the headstone where they'd gathered and pushed their way up to obliterate the words on the stone. The dirty marks they left saddened her. She felt an urge to grab a scrubbing brush and clean the life out of it but that would simply etch the name and epitaph deeper into her mind.

She looked at it now. Mark Reid, born 18 January 1969 died 5 October 2003. Died as he lived - riding the waves of life.

The years had both flown by and dragged. In the early days she knew she'd missed days, nights, weeks at a time. They had simply melted from her mind amidst the tears and aching. Jen had called, visited her. She knew because her mum had told her. But she had no recollection.

"You told her you'd be all right. You hugged her. You both cried. You even had a drink together. A night out at the Standard. You were both pissed, exhausted with crying. I wish I had taken a photo of you, propping each other up. You looked like sisters again," her mum said.

Sisters again. The rain pelted the ground around her, drilling into her shoulders, stinging her face when it swirled around. The weather had been like this the day of the accident.

Jen had phoned early that day to postpone the trip to the ranges.

"It's a bad forecast, squally showers and possible hail."

"We're all set though. Mags has got the kids, she's doing us a huge favour. We can't really pull out now. Besides, since when did the Bureau get weather forecasts right?"

She can still hear how she sounded. So righteous, selfish really. She was determined, at any cost, to go on the outing. She had begged Mags to look after the children. She had planned the child-free day for so long that nothing would stand in her way.

"Well, I'm not sure. I just think it'll be a wasted day if we're all huddled under trees shivering." Jen's words passed over her. She couldn't have cared less.

The sun broke through the barrelling grey clouds an hour into the ride. Jen conceded defeat and laughed when the boys revved hard and skidded around them whipping up mud and leaf litter.

Now, in the pelting rain she could feel that mud and debris again, she could smell the petrol fumes, she could hear the throaty gurgle of the motors running and then the engines screaming off down the tracks. Ice trickled down her spine. She'd relived it so many times but here in front of the grave, with his name staring back at her, the memory of the noise, the mangling metal, the whining of the engine, the wheels still spinning, a moment of pure silence, then the screaming.

Somewhere behind her the man with the wheelbarrow was raking up leaves again. Sunlight, a faded silver, washed across the sky. She moved forward, touched the cool stone of the grave.

"I'm sorry, Mark. So sorry."

The tears tracked down her face. Memories filled her mind's eye. Babies in bathtubs, a wedding gown hanging against the wardrobe door, huge Tiger prawns on the hotplate, the pop of a Champagne cork, the smell of his hair.

She didn't know how long she stayed there. She only became aware again when pain registered and she released her fingers and pulled her bloodied palms from her pockets. It was a release from the real pain, the ache that never left. She imagined it like a second heart beating inside her, expanding and contracting, reminding her of her humanity, her vitality. She needed to feel its throbbing. Just to remind her each day of what she had done.

The man with the wheelbarrow stopped in front of her. "It'll be better the next time you're here. Mother Nature has spoken but we tend not to listen to her for very long." He smiled. They're always in your heart, aren't they? Lost ones." He picked up the handles of the barrow and walked it back to the pile of debris.

She scrunched her hands in her pockets again, the rawness of her palms keeping her focused.

"Always in your heart." The voice hadn't changed. And why would it? Jen was Jen however much space there had been between them.

Madeleine turned and saw her sister. In front of her sat Connor, Jen's son. The wheels of his chair were grimy with mud and gravel. He was holding flowers on his lap.

"Hey," Jen whispered.

"Hey. How are you?" A whoosh of blood rushed to her ears. What right had she to ask?

"Better for seeing you. I knew you'd be here. I woke up this morning and just knew."

Rain fell again, softer this time. "Ten years. I had to come. And the storm."

"Yes, the storm." Jen looked around at the workers beavering away. "What a way to commemorate."

"It's a mess." She knelt in front of the wheelchair. "Shall I put these on the grave for you?"

Connor didn't move. His face hung in the same expression as it had when she saw him hooked up to the machines in hospital. Slack mouth, one eye more open than the other, one ear crushed against his head.

Jen nodded. "A real mess. It's always been a mess."

A month after the accident Madeleine found Jen slumped over Connor's bed. Grey faced, red eyed, unchanged. Bleeps, Darth Vader sounds from the ventilator, flashing numbers everywhere. It was hot, a sapping heat that made you feel nauseous. Madeleine sat in the corner. How different their world had become. Jen's husband Mark was dead, her son Connor a vegetable. Madeleine's husband Andrew had survived. Not a scratch. They had gone home to their girls and life was the same.

It was all her fault. She'd pushed for it, she'd insisted. She'd wrecked her sister's family for a day without kids. And she knew from that moment she could not remain Jen's sister. She could not remain a mother to her children. She could not remain a wife. It was that simple. She had to leave. And she did.

"I brought photos of the kids," Jen said, fishing an envelope out of her bag. "Would you like to see them?"

The familiarity of her voice infiltrated something buried deep within. Photos of Hannah and Carly. Faces she hadn't seen for ten years. Hair she hadn't stroked, cheeks she hadn't kissed, hands she hadn't squeezed. She took the envelope.

"I do understand why you punished yourself like you did, Maddie. But the girls have never understood. They love you. They hate you. But most of all they miss you. It's not too late. It will never be too late. Come back to us."

Connor laughed. It was a shock, amongst the grief and the storm damage.

"I miss them too but they deserve so much more."

Jen took from the bag hooped over the back of his chair a small pink plush kitten. Madeleine gasped. Hannah's Blue, named that because she had wanted a blue one to set it apart from the ones Carly had been given when she was born. Blue was matted and twisted but despite its grizzled appearance it tugged at her heart, her memories.

She was still holding the flowers. She placed them on the grave. She turned back to Connor and took the kitten. She held it to her face. The smell of her children was caught in the fur. She inhaled.

Jen ruffled Connor's hair. He grunted. "They deserve their mother, broken or otherwise. Think about, Maddie. If not for them, for me."

The wheels turned and scrunched over the ground and she listened until she couldn't hear them anymore.

Effie Merryl

I stood outside in the backyard by the coal bunker trying not to see the black dust and grey grime and moss crawling green up the bricks. I was trying not to think about the outside lav and the odious smells as they curdled up my nose, weaving a path into my sinuses. I had such a heightened sense of smell, it was knocking me sick.

It was then I should have realised. It was always a give-away, a tell-tale sign. But when I saw the blood, relief swept through me. Not this month. Thank the lord. Not this month. And never again, I hoped. If only he'd keep away from me like that. I kept telling him to be careful but he was having none of it.

Ten days later I was stood outside by the odious lav again. The rain was pat-pattering down on my head. I blew smoke rings up into the dank air as cold sea-frets curdled around me, wafting in from the slippery rock shore. I watched the slow circular halos disperse into the heavy air and I had that feeling again. Something wasn't right. I thought about my rumbling tummy, the constant heartburn, the sickening smells and the feeling I had on waking up, the feeling like I needed to vomit. I knew I was short-tempered too but then I was always short-tempered so maybe the temper wasn't a sign, it was just me. Not that I'd ever admit it to the man.

I smoothed down me pinny, fumbled in the front pocket for another match, and lit up the soggy fag again because the rain had put it out. What the feck was I gonna do?

Another kid. An extra mouth on my tit. Just got one off, still had one on, couldn't be doing with another. I felt like one of those factory conveyor belts, one off, one on, one off, one on. I tried hard to think of it as a baby, a growing living thing inside me, another little me. Or another little him. We already had six of the buggers and the eldest was about to turn nine. There was only so much money, so much porridge and forage, only so much I could do with a five time or more hand-me-down. An' I was forever shouting at the kids, yelling to wait for their father to get home. He'd sort 'em out, either give 'em a belt or a tanner.

I was knackered and ready for the boards. And me only thirty four, too. Lank hair with no curl, a flabby baby belly, and tits I could sling under me armpits. I don't need no other bairn. No more kids.

I went down to the dispensary in Arcmanger Lane every few days asking for something for the dyspepsia, something for the sickness, something for my foul bad temper. I also asked for something for my old man to stop me getting in the family way. I took everything they gave me and more. I took anything I could think of to make it go away, to stop it from growing inside me. To get rid. It was a bit like I was committing a murder but not because it wasn't here yet, alive and kicking, not breathing. Not really anything at all. That's how I made myself think.

Nothing worked so I tried to think of it as a baby but then I couldn't. It was a thing. Just a growing thing inside me. Like a real live bairn but I couldn't help think of it like one of them yet, with its own face, own features, own personality.

Everywhere I went I had to take the bairns with me and I couldn't manage another. I really couldn't. I was never maternal before I had 'em but I did look after them and I was a proud mam an' all that. I did me best. It just got me mad these days because I never had a minute to sit down and I was knackered like an auld horse every minute of every day. And I was especially fed up with the tits I could sling under me armpits that weren't attractive anymore and not pert and up and round and sexy like Pat what's-her-name over the way that I saw me old man looking at when he thought I wasn't looking at him.

Every night I'd wake up and lie sweating with fear about another mouth on my nipple, the red stuck-out berry that wouldn't smooth down like it did when I was sixteen. I'd feel that little mouth sucking at me, draining me dry. I imagined it taking all the life from me and gorging itself on my red-red blood. Then I'd open me eyes to it and it was all a nightmare and I'd be having those night sweats again.

I could do nothing else but see the doctor. Get sorted with it and start to prepare. Time would be here soon enough and I would have to tell him, the old man, that there'd be another mouth to feed. Another one of us. Another conglomeration of me and him. And of course, he'd go on the piss for three days to celebrate another drain on our meagre existence.

When I finally went to see the Doc, my prayers to the lord had been answered. Sort of. There was no baby. No baby at all. And I thought, for one brief minute, the smallest time possible, that it was all okay, and relief flooded through me, up from my toes making them tingle. I thought for the flicker of a few seconds that it would all be all right.

But it was not all right. It was worse. There was no baby. Never had been a baby. Not this time. Babbies no more. It wasn't a baby at all but it was a definite living thing growing inside me. It was the hugest tumour the doctor had ever known. So he said.

After lots of those horrible tests, and the poking and the scans and the examinations at the hospital, they said there was nothing to be done. It was still growing inside me and after a few months there would be no birth, no mouth on my tit, no combination of me and him a-squealing and a-squawking. And I wished I could take it all back to when I stood in the backyard making smoke rings and thinking about names for me baby that never was and wishing it wasn't. I wished it was a baby, saggy tits and all, but there would be no more lullabies.

This thing I had growing inside would be the death of me.

BLUE WIDOW

EILIDH THOMAS

Widow...
You have a name
A persona, a past
Fragmented stories of tinctures
In blue

Beneath
Your tears, a bird
Framed and plumed from your heart
Guards an undue sarcophagus
Of loss

Shadow
Upon shadow
Retreats into darkness
Stony-faced skin over bone hides
Wild thoughts

Behind...
Veiled in reproach
A nameless woman grieves
Her destiny, and madness gropes
For light

Handfast
Woes with kindness
Twisted love lies falsely
Old horizons in decay, fade
And die

Eyes gaze...
Contemptuous
Of sadness. Where to now?
There is no final answer, but
silence.

PATIENCE

FRANCIS HAYES

she waits at the railway station
for a train that never arrives

the sleepers rot on the gravel
the rails are red, pitted with rust

when the last train left the station
she watched the red lamp bob and sway

she saw the two parallel trails
streak behind like a jet exhaust -
foreshadowing the rust on the track

she knew then hope was all in vain -
like the candle in her window
she lights before leaving her home

DOUGLAS PUGH

Dylan cursed.

The unfamiliar living room of his grandparents' house held not only all manner of strange furniture, with their odd textures and protruding angles, but numerous recumbent forms. Relatives snoring beneath borrowed blankets, a couple of smaller cousins huddled up under one of grannies voluminous fur coats. The sounds of sleeping helped place some of the edges to avoid in the darkness, but others - like the brutal edge of the coffee table that he had just found – were silent and solid, crashing against the delicacies of shin bones.

'Shhhhhhhhhhhhhhhh!'

Dylan rubbed his bruised shin, felt around the coffee table and trod carefully around it. The rectangle of dim light that betrayed the window in the back door was his only real guide and at least he was getting closer.

His stomach churned once more and he stifled a belch as best he could, wincing at the acrid taste.

With relations, of course, came assumptions, seemingly the more remote the relation the more assuming they were of expected expertise.

'From Norwich, ain't you? East Anglia, flat as a fart round there.'

'Nantwich actually, it's in Cheshire.'

'Cheshire?' Dylan had seen one relative after another computing the answer, 'Cheese and cats, innit?'

'It's actually lovely countryside wedged between Manchester and Liverpool ...'

'Oh countryside ...'

Which the relatives then extrapolated into Dylan and his parents being expert on things remotely rural, and promptly fielded them with all sorts of questions about woodcraft, animal husbandry and the black art of 'growing things'.

Dylan had tried to explain that Nantwich, and Stoke where he worked, were not quite countryside. That they were pretty much urban dwellers and only drove through the countryside, but their fate was set.

And there was the other assumption.

'You're a Goldstone, lad. Goldstone's love jellied eels. Always have, always will. Get 'em down you.'

His own assumption had been that he would get used to them.

Which was why at God-only-knows-what-time-in-the-morning he was trying to get outside for some fresh air. His roommates – vague cousins – had insisted.

As Dylan sighed in relief upon actually getting his hand on the handle of the back door his guts rebelled again and he clenched at his stomach and groaned.

'Shhhhhhhhhhhhhh!'

Try as he might Dylan could no longer contain himself and he let loose an immense fart before deftly slipping out of the door onto the patio, closing off all responses of 'Bloody hell!' and 'Oh, my Go...'

The night air was beautifully cool and leaning against the brickwork of his grandparents' house, Dylan felt the sweat from his forehead evaporating away. He reminded himself to make a very strong mental note to avoid jellied eels at all costs for the rest of his life, Goldstone or not.

The commotion behind him in the house had died slowly down, and even though the effects of the air were starting to lean more towards chilly, Dylan had no inclination to go back indoors. There had to be nearly forty of the Goldstone clan here in his grandparents' house and it was good to actually get time and space alone. The relatives of course would put it down to him being a country bumpkin.

Dylan though had made assumptions himself. To his own mind this gathering was in London, a teeming city of skyscrapers and millions of people living around the clock underneath bright lights, small streets and too many cars.

Yet he had seen no skyscrapers. There were the odd tower block apartments here in Middlesex but no total smothering of the skyline with endless brick. Why if you looked at the night sky you could almost make out what? Six stars?

The irony was that his own assumption had people stacked up everywhere in a big city yet here he was at his grandparents house for their fiftieth anniversary bash in a house crammed full of people.

He pushed himself away from the house, the brickwork feeling too cold and too coarse against his skin.

As he did so he thought he detected some movement down in the depths of grandad's garden.

Dylan screwed his eyes up and peered into the inky depths, past the fading lawn and between the larch lap fence and the vegetable patch.

He only had to wait a few seconds and something down there moved again.

He recalled grandad saying something about 'Bloody rabbits in my veggies' and seeking advice, but this was far bigger than any rabbit Dylan had ever seen.

He waited and the rustling of something down in the vegetable plot came again.

Dylan stooped down low and crept carefully along the flagstones of the pathway, thankfully a straight line so that he could follow it even as it faded into the darkness. He was glad that he'd come out in only his stockinged feet though that might be tricky if he had to dash across any of the dug earth or grass.

The rustling came again and from his new vantage point Dylan could make out a small figure outlined against the garden shed. This was no rabbit!

He hesitated. Should he just yell at this interloper and scare them off? Should he creep back to the house and get help?

It was only a small figure after all. A child perhaps, but at this time of night? Maybe it was even one of his many cousins, but if so what on earth were they doing in the veggie patch?

Dylan had an idea. He thrust his hand into his trouser pocket and closed it around his mobile phone. If he flipped it open the light should be just enough to make out detail close up, something that he had used in one or two dingy pub car parks to find his way. If he kept it closed until the last second it would carry an element of surprise too.

Feeling somewhat braver with something of a 'weapon' in his hand, Dylan crept step by stealthy step down the garden path, pausing every time the figure stopped. He could make out two small glinting white eyes in the dark now and noticed a most definite action of sniffing the air loudly every time that it became cautious. A curious action and certainly not something that he would expect any family member to do.

When he had closed the gap to about twenty feet Dylan realised that he was going to have to go off the path, and that route would take him across the orderly rows of vegetables. He could only rush at the figure, flip the phone open and make a grab for them. This constant stooping low was starting to cramp muscles in his legs and back so the sooner he did it the better.

The creature (Person? Child?) bobbed up and down in a rhythmic fashion, stopping from time to time to sniff the air and look around with its bright little eyes, and then dining noisily on whatever it had extracted from grandad's garden. Every now and then it made little noises that were perhaps words, talking quietly to itself though Dylan could not clearly discern any words.

Dylan decided that he had to rush out when its head was down, perhaps yelling some choice words for added impact. He bunched his legs and rushed.

'Oi!!!' he yelled as he thudded across the soft soil, flicked open the mobile phone and launched himself rugby tackle-style in a diving grab.

He saw wide, pale eyes and a horror stricken look on a face that was centred around a dirt smeared mouth and a carrot grasped between teeth and hands. The mobile phone was dropped as he thudded into the vegetable thief and his hands grasped at clothing.

The figure set off a wailing and a hissing racket, showing amazing strength for such a small person. It frantically tried to literally tear itself from Dylan's grasp, as clothing tore asunder as it thrashed and wriggled away from him.

The struggle rolled across the rows of vegetables and suddenly the twosome were thudding into the side of the garden shed, not only popping the door open, but causing an almighty ruckus of falling things inside the shed too judging by the noise.

Still the two battled, Dylan trying to use his size and weight, the intruder showing alarming strength and agility. Twice in the space of seconds it seemed to have broken free from Dylan's grasp only for him to find another handhold just as it verged on escape. The third time it let its jacket slip off its arms and burst forth only for Dylan to stretch out a lunging leg and trip it, sending it crashing head first into the shed itself. Dylan dived in after it and pulled the door closed, dropping the latch as he did so.

He fumbled up and down the sides of the door, cussed as he found a splinter, and then felt relieved as he found and threw a light switch.

A black rag and a pair of bony, well grimed bare feet stuck out from beneath a bench. Already bruised and pumped up with the excitement of the fight, Dylan grabbed the ankles and dragged the creature out, ignoring the whimpers and moans.

The creature seemed to be a small boy of maybe ten or eleven years of age, garbed only in threadbare black trousers that were ragged and much frayed. It shielded its eyes from the light with both its hands and the flapping remnants of its once white shirt. Dylan was struck not only by the ancient style of the clothing but also by the dirt that was so grimed into both hands and feet that it appeared to be part of the skin itself. He also noted with a bit of caution that the nails on both hands and feet were both long and sharp, more talon than nail.

'So, we meet at last.' Dylan loomed over the small figure, hoping to menace it with his bulk and size. He wanted no more fighting. 'Who are you?'

The creature continued to do nothing more than make whimpering and keening noises, curling itself into a ball as much as it could.

'I can wait all night if you insist.'

The whimpering stopped suddenly and with a sniff the creature pried its fingers apart ever so slightly.

'Till brightnessss comesss?' it asked.

'Oh ho, so you can talk!' smiled Dylan. This was progress at last. 'Brightness comes? You mean like dawn? Sure, I can wait longer than that. My family will be coming then.'

The whimpering started all over again and the creature covered its eyes again.

'Look, for Christ's sake, stop all this crying. It won't help.'

The boy suddenly uncoiled and dashed for the door, thudding heavily into the wood and nearly bursting it open. Dylan made a grab for the ankles to haul it away and the boy twisted and turned – once more with astonishing strength – and finally snapped its teeth at Dylan's hands, dragging two large scratches down the back of one of them.

'Son of a bitch!'

The boy huddled against the doorpost, squashed in a corner against an old humming freezer and hissing and snapping at Dylan with incisors that could only be...

'Jesus! You're a vampire.'

The boy hissed and spit at him again, and this time Dylan decided that he was not getting any closer if he could help it. He found an old fork in the corner of the shed and thrust it at the boy.

'So that's why you don't want the brightness to come, eh? Burns don't it?'

In his head Dylan was figuring that he maybe had a couple of hours to go until dawn. This was going to be a long night.

The impasse of fang and fork soon grew boring for the pair of them. The boy stopped hissing and spitting, Dylan found his arms growing weary from holding the fork.

'Not vampire.'

'No? Then the teeth are from a costume shop then are they? And what's a vampire want with my grandad's carrots?'

'Isss forager.'

'Forager? Never heard of them.'

'Ssssssometimessss they ssssays vegpire, but we likesss forager bestssss.'

'Vegpire? Is that like a vampire but you like vegetables?'

'Vampires' bad cousins. They likessss suck you dry, you ooomans.'

Dylan laughed.

'You don't scare me, that's just that Hollywood rubbish.'

'Yessss?'

The boy started making regular high pitched calls, moving his mouth and making sounds that Dylan could barely make out. He jabbed the kid with the fork.

'Oi! What you doing?'

'I call family. Maybe cousinssss come. No?' The pinched, filthy face tilted and looked at Dylan mischievously.

Dylan responded with a firmer jab of the fork. 'No!'

Both eyed each other in silence again.

'Why do you want my grandad's veggies anyway? There's loads of 'em in the countryside. Fields and fields ...'

The boy twisted his face in distaste and spat.

'Pesssticides, niii -trates, phossssssphates, 'ormonesssssss. Ach! No veggies, isss chemicalsss with leaveses.'

'Whereas here .... they're organics, aren't they?'

The boy smiled, his fangs prominent over his dirt ringed mouth.

'Well, I'll be damne ...'

The boy suddenly leapt upwards on top of the freezer, cleared away a clatter of flowerpots and smashed through the dusty window that lay behind them. The freezer tumbled over knocking the fork out of Dylan's hands and then spilling its contents all over him.

Dylan pushed the cold, hard lumps off himself and clambered to his feet, getting up just in time to see the black feet wriggle out of the window.

'You little bastard!'

Casting his eyes around Dylan looked for some sort of weapon, there just had to be something that would do. He tossed away bags of peas, broccoli, frozen bread.

'Of course ...' Dylan grabbed his weapon of choice and burst through the shed door in hot pursuit. Lights were already coming on in the grandparents' house and it would only be a matter of minutes before he had a lot to explain.

The vegpire was scrabbling its way over the top of the fence when Dylan grabbed it and dragged it back down. Winded it lay flat on its back until it saw what was in his hand.

'Nooooo!' it wailed.

Dylan struck, just like they did in the Hollywood movies. He ignored the iciness of his weapon and the fact that where he held it was becoming a little squishy. Straight to the heart.

The vegpire wailed and suddenly vapourised into dust.

By the time Dylan had caught his breath the family surrounded him, barraged him with questions.

'A fox, ' he explained.

'Got away,' he explained.

'In my hand? Oh, that's just the very best steak,' he explained.

Which had to be better than jellied eels.

AFTER SCHOOL

JOSS HAYES

I trudge home
zig-zagging uphill
leather satchel strap
cutting my shoulder
swirls of mist a unicorn's breath
magic droplets trapped
in my hair
a weasel on a sandstone stile
fixes me with black bead eyes
I stare at her
blink
and she's gone.

EILIDH THOMAS

There isn't much time left. Evan and Claire will be here soon and I must be away. I don't want our paths to cross ever again.

Kristina would have been upset at the disarray in her house. But she's no longer here to do anything about it. She just upped sticks and went back to Slovenia. Not that I blame her, the way Evan had been messing about for years. She'd put up with a lot.

Evan and Kristina had met as students. She was in Bristol for a year on an exchange from her home town of Rožna Dolina on the Italian border, to improve her English and teach Italian. Evan was totally smitten, pursued her relentlessly until she said yes – to marriage. Kristina didn't have time to waste on a student romance.

Greig and I didn't see them much in the early years after university. Later on, once the children arrived, we visited more often, but mostly all of us had too much to do with work and family.

At least Greig and I wanted family. Kristina wasn't so sure and Evan made no comment. Kristina said there were plenty of children in the world and she saw enough of them at school. As soon as she could, she packed her twins off to childminders or on long holidays to her family in Slovenia, and when they were old enough, to boarding school.

It's a waste of time reminiscing. Soon they will be out of our life forever. No more reminders of what had been with every visit to the house. Much has changed there anyway in a short space of time – in the clutter of furniture, in the additions of flowery curtains, and in the appearance of useless knickknacks about the place – not exactly tasteless but not as stylish as it had once been. A lot has stayed the same, of course – the children's photos on the wall, books on the shelves, and the beds. They could have bought new beds. You would think a new woman would want that at least.

Kristina's career had taken off when she became head of department. She was totally immersed in her job with conferences and meetings, and she was good too. She could get money out a stone for the smallest school in her jurisdiction. But, oh dear, sometimes she would bore me half to death with stories about work. We got on well enough though. It's not always easy to befriend your husband's friend's wife. It takes a bit more work.

Evan had his own interests at the yacht club, organising regattas and generally promoting himself and his construction business. His father had been a joiner. He had inherited the small business from him and grew it very quickly into a smart housing development company. It was a boom time for everyone, and as a couple Evan and Kristina were asked to all the local social occasions in the town. That is until Evan was caught *in flagrante* with the local florist's wife. It appeared that their marriage was not the bed of roses everyone had thought.

Kristina seemed to shrug off the whole episode very quickly. We heard rumours, of course, even at a distance. Their partying and jet-setting life style grew and it seemed the *faux pas* was soon forgotten. Then to our surprise they decided they would buy a second home along the coast not far from us. We joked about it – how we could catch up properly again and how good it would be to meet on a regular basis. Time yet to recapture our youth we said.

I'm not exactly sure when things started to get uncomfortable. Perhaps the routine we had all fallen into created its own tensions. Every month or so Evan and Kristina would spend a long weekend at their holiday home and we would visit each other turn about. Perhaps it was when Kristina's Slovenian family started to take holidays with them or business friends joined them as a sweetener for a contract. Perhaps it was when Claire came to stay, occasionally sharing their weekend away.

Even when all the unpleasant business first blew up, Evan still wanted someone to look in at the house when it was empty, although I often wondered if he remembered he had asked us to do so. It all seems pointless now, like being left with someone's dog when they apparently couldn't care less.

I decided a while back not to pick up the post on any of my visits to the house even though a pile of junk mail on the floor looks untidy. When I spoke to the couple across the lane they said they had returned their set of keys. No need to ask why, but I couldn't stop them elaborating at length, regardless. It's a small village after all.

Greig and I had gone to look at houses with Evan and Kristina when the notion had first come into their heads that they would like a second home. Evan had lined up viewings for several properties over a weekend. They stayed with us that time, as they had done occasionally, even though Evan's sister lived only ten miles away. There was some unpleasantness in the family past so they kept their distance from each other.

As soon as Kristina walked into the house she fell in love with it. It had been completely refurbished with all new fittings and a large open plan living area – most unexpected in a seatown house. She didn't want anything that would turn into another project for Evan. I was quite taken with the place myself, except it had no view, apart from one from the back door. A small conservatory extension and a bit of new decking would soon fix that, Evan said quietly out of earshot from Kristina.

On their early visits to the house, Evan and Kristina often brought us gifts, some very extravagant from their foreign holidays, which was a bit embarrassing – rugs from Turkey, silk wall hangings from India, and a set of bronze replica figures of the Terracotta Warriors from China. Others were more the usual – a bottle of wine and a box of fancy biscuits and cheese. Once they brought a bottle of Goldschlager, which after one drink made me feel ill for days. I'm sure the tiny flakes of gold in it had cut up my liver.

Another small gift they brought sat in the cupboard unopened for long enough, *Claire's Handmade Plum Jam*. Evan made such a fuss about it and the quality of the produce made by Claire, who had started a business in her kitchen from scratch when her husband left her and she had no income. At that time I use to make a lot of jam myself so the jar was easily forgotten at the back of the cupboard. I came across it again recently and put it straight into the bin, unopened. It was past its sell by date anyway.

There was one particularly lovely time, a perfect midsummer's day, when everyone, including the children, arrived for the weekend. Greig and I decided we would host a BBQ, bring the two families together for an afternoon and evening. It turned into one of those iconic memories. Everyone happy, everyone getting on with each other, the food was great and the weather perfect. We sat outside until almost midnight sipping drinks and watching the sun set over the water, drop down behind the dark islands of the bay. Claire was there too, blending in seamlessly with the company. One of Evan and Kristina's twins had a new partner, the other was just back from a year out in New Zealand. Our two girls had their own excitement, respectively preparing for the eldest's wedding and the youngest's graduation.

I stood for a while watching the party from our conservatory door, absorbing the picture and thinking how this moment would stay with me forever. Kristina stared back at me from her distant perch on the garden wall and raised her glass in a toast. Evan and Claire were deep in conversation on the swing hammock while Greig attended to the food and drink. The younger generation lounged around chatting like this was the life that they were made for. The laughter and shared stories seemed endless. Then the taxi arrived and our guests departed.

Soon afterwards the economic bubble burst, along with a downturn in Evan's construction business, so their house is still waiting for its extension.

At first it was Greig who would check the house in between visits from Evan and Kristina. He was always out and about with work more than I, so it made sense. When I started a night class in a nearby school, I was left with the task, a thankless one as it turned out, for over a year.

After that, whatever caused it, things changed. As suddenly as they had appeared, Evan and Kristina stopped visiting.

From time to time Greig or I would give them a call to let them know how things were with their house. One time I arrived to find a cat sitting on the bed in the spare room. The lock on the cat flap, which had been installed by the last occupants, was broken, and a very large ginger Tom had made himself quite comfortable on the bed. The cat bolted as soon as it saw me. Greig went over and taped up the offending flap with duck tape. A report to Evan on the incident was met with a polite thank you and little else.

Some time later Greig tried Evan and Kristina's home phone number and it came up as disconnected. Their mobile phones no longer worked either. I went onto Google to discover their family home of over thirty years was up for sale. By this time we hadn't seen them for six months. We were guessing at the problems. They had been a bit glum on their last visit. Perhaps Evan's business was in deeper trouble than we thought. Perhaps the family was having difficulties or for some other reason they were making the move to Slovenia that Kristina always wanted.

Finally, Greig phoned Evan's office and was relieved to find he was at least still in business. It took a number of calls though, before we got the whole story, or Evan's version of the whole story. Yes, Kristina had moved to Slovenia, and Evan, he had moved into a flat with Claire. The shock was immense and yet the signals had been there for long enough. I felt I should get in touch with Kristina, after all we had known each other a long time, but Evan blocked my inquiries for contact details, saying she didn't want to speak to anyone from her old life.

Greig took all this from Evan with a degree of ambivalence and indifference, which I found puzzling. They had been friends almost since school. It felt as though Kristina had been air-brushed out and Claire air-brushed in without any farewells, explanations, or a quiet drink in the pub to ease the way. Evan said a lot of people no longer spoke to him, not even his daughter, and his son only grudgingly. He wasn't too happy about that and concluded time would heal all. I thought he was being more than a bit optimistic. As to whether it had been worth it, he said it had been difficult.

I locked the door of their house for the last time, stuck the keys into an envelope with a note from Greig to Evan before I pushed the envelope through the letter box. I felt a momentary twinge of sadness, then breathed a sigh of relief and skipped along the beach chasing the wind. Perhaps this change was a good thing after all.

FRANCIS HAYES

October, conkers month for all right thinking English boys; girls too for all I know. But I didn't know then and I certainly don't know now.

The leaves start to fall and the first one you learn to identify is the five finger spread of the horse chestnut. Then you learn that that among the golden brown carpet at the foot of the tree nestles the pale green hedgehog spiked seed case that hides the glossy brown sphere, the conker.

The risks we took for those little brown nuts; and all so we could pierce them, lace them on a string and bray hell out of our neighbour's conker until bonfire night, when conker season was all over for another year. We would run, heedless of the traffic, to gather the new fallen fruit from the road, climb, ignoring wind and rain, to gather the fruit from the branches before it fell. We trespassed.

The best conkers in our village came from the trees in the estate of New Cotham Hall.

For twelve years after the war the Hall stood empty. The word was that the Cotham family had been wiped out. The males perished in battles which were the legends handed down to us. The women and children were buried in the wreckage of a bombed out mansion in London.

The Hall stood unoccupied. Behind the shuttered windows and the massive oak door it was like the Marie Celeste, village rumour said. Food rotted in the pantry, champagne corks popped in the cellars, laundry waited the wash, toys were strewn across the nursery floor where they had lain when the house was shut up on the eve of the eldest daughter's coming of age.

Tenant farmers still grazed the land, sowing crops which they gathered in due season and paying rent to a firm of solicitors in London. The parkland around the house deteriorated, reverting to meadow and woodland, unchecked. The horse chestnuts flourished. Every October small gangs of village children descended on the parkland to gather conkers that would vanquish the poor specimens gathered by their peers from the neighbouring villages on the playgrounds of their schools.

Then in October of nineteen fifty eight when the village boys went to enter the park we found that the rusted iron gates no longer stood open. They were painted a shade of dull green and locked firmly against us. The sign that had always warned us 'Dogs Patrol The Grounds,' that we knew to be a wooden lie had been repainted. The letters stood out stark white and square in a typeface reminiscent of the London underground's typeface against a background the same dull green as the gates were painted.

We peered through to see where the dogs were but saw none.

We walked along the road and down the lane beside the estate. Where there were gaps in the thorny hedgerow we saw bright new fencing, tall, topped with barbed wire that glittered evilly in the October sun.

Billy Clark had a plan.

'You have to lay something over the wire so it don't stick you. My dad was a commando in the war. He told me that.'

'It must have to be thick.'

'A mattress would do it.'

'Where would we get a mattress?'

Billy knew. Stealing a mattress seemed like a heinous crime but Billy explained.

'There's one lying in old Ken Stone's back garden. Been there weeks. I expect he's planning on burning it on bonfire night then burying the springs under his runner beans.'

'Under his runner beans?'

'Works a treat. Conditions the soil. The metal rust's down. Didn't you know?'

Those that didn't said nothing, just stored this knowledge away for future reference. Those who knew had nothing to add except to wonder how we might get hold of the mattress.

'Easy,' said Billy. 'Over our wall into Ken's garden, lift it into mine, down our back path across the allotment and up the road. We'll get it back to Ken the same way.'

'When?'

'Sooner the better if we want the best conkers. Tonight.'

'We can't get conkers in the dark.'

'We'll leave the mattress in here.' He pointed to the gap between the hedge and the fence. 'We'll come back tomorrow afternoon and pop over the fence. Then we'll get the mattress back to Ken's tomorrow night.'

'But how do we get out of our house?' Several of us asked.

That's your problem. We'll need three at least. Two to carry the mattress, one for a look-out. More would be batter.'

Then he dropped the bombshell.

'Those that don't come can't go over the fence. That's fair.'

It was fair. We didn't argue.

Then someone said, 'What about the dogs?' We'd been so taken up with getting over the fence we hadn't thought about the dogs.

'I'll bet there are none,' said Billy. 'There's always been a sign and we've never seen any dogs.'

'There were none when we looked through the gate, neither.'

So we forgot about the dogs.

It wasn't easy getting out of the house at half past nine that night. I don't suppose it was for the others but at the time I didn't give it much thought.

Six of us turned up to manhandle the mattress from Ken Stone's garden to the Hall. Six of us turned up next afternoon to throw the mattress over the wire.

Billy went first, stepping up in the cupped hands of two of us. That was when we realised that probably at least one of us would have to stay outside the fence. Faces fell. Bill had to go over; it was his plan and in a sense it was his mattress. We dipped for it, 'Ip dip, sky blue, who's it, not you.' That was as far as we needed to do. 'Not you, said it all. It was not me so I helped each one over then stood by the fence waiting, rewarded with a promise of equal division of the spoils to keep everything fair.

I heard the barking. If loudness was an indicator then these were big dogs; three of them I guessed. I heard the shouting although I could not make out the words.

I heard Billy scream, high, drawn out and ending in a strangled yelp then silence. I heard Tom Vale yell for help; that was all I heard. John Ferris appeared out of the undergrowth, running to the fence, then he stumbled and fell in the grass. I saw a blurred grey shape spring from the brush and leap to where John had fallen then I saw no more.

They recovered the bodies of Peter Morson and Michael Grant from behind the wrought iron gates. They might have escaped if the gates had not been locked; but then if the gates were not locked the dogs would not have been loose, the solicitor for the owners explained to the inquest.

When the coroner's officer interviewed me he only asked, 'Did you see the sign?'

I said I had. He asked, 'Can you read?'

'Yes.'

'Did you understand it?'

'Yes,' I said, 'But -'

'No buts,' he said. So I never got to tell him about the wooden lie.

DARK DISSONANCE

DOUGLAS PUGH

you digest
the sultry timbres of Cohen
in the dark, slicking your skin
with his voice, his words

you bathe in his depths
while I am ripping
guitar solos, on a Highway to Hell
trilling trebles, blowing bass

I am past asking
'How was it for you?' because
the answer
to a question, maybe not heard,
drowns in our dissonance

that place where there is no sound
no words, not even
the sound of lapping
and these days neither of us drink
from that bowl

perhaps would not care
for the reflections,
you stippled in ego and literacy
while I, slip sliding
to carnal primitive

may not even see what I see

you clothe sated skin with
smug quotes, I am stretching to grasp
my insides, ride my urges

and neither of us
is reaching for a light switch

are we?

COMMON GROUND

GILL TERRY

Drum rolls polluted the night air
on that Lakenheath to Libya junket.
Awake in a bed, not a bender,
I counted them out and back.

Next day I took offerings to Green Gate
toilet rolls, tea bags, a ten pound note
this ephemeral spineless Sister
sidestepping the worst of the mud.

What legacy did they leave, then,
these women who embraced the base
with coloured scarves and baby clothes
defied the nuclear threat with dancing?

Still of special scientific interest
these days lapwing and nightjar
and Joni Mitchell's butterflies
deploy above the Common's yellow gorse.

But gang rapists post their videos online
politicians award themselves peace prizes
and bulldozers, uncontested, raze a Camp's memorial garden
from the corner of a British field.

*(On hearing that the Greenham Common Women's Peace Camp
Commemorative Site has been demolished by the owners of the business
park that now occupies the former military base.)*

Joss Hayes

'Mum,' said Thomas, 'Oliver's got a dog.'

Liz, Thomas's mother, looked at him over her glasses. 'A toy one?'

'No. A real one. He says it stinks.'

'Well, he's telling whoppers. Or maybe he's just winding you up? His mummy wouldn't have got a dog without telling me. She knows how you feel about dogs. I'm sure you're mistaken, darling.'

Thomas's bottom lip trembled. 'He has got a dog. He doesn't tell fibs. Fibbers aren't nice people. You said. So I can't go to his house any more. Not tonight. Not ever.' Tears gathered in the corners of Thomas's eyes.

Liz slowly shook her head. 'Oh, Thomas,' she said. 'Is that what this is all about? You don't want to go to Oliver's? But you usually like going to Ollie's.'

'I do. I want to go. But I'm not going if he's got a dog.'

Thomas's mother sighed. She looked around for the phone, picked it up from the coffee table and began texting with both thumbs. Thomas wiped his face with the heel of his hand, smearing a greyish streak across his cheek bone. He sniffed. After a few moments Liz put the phone down and smiled at her son. 'Well that's O.K., then. There is no dog. So you have nothing to worry about. You can go to Ollie's house while I go to college. No problem.'

Thomas still looked dubious. 'But, Mum, he told us about his dog. He really did. This morning, at school.'

'I expect you misheard, or misunderstood. Does he perhaps have an imaginary dog? Some children have imaginary friends, you know. I had a pet goat when I was little, but it wasn't real. I just used to make up stories about it.'

Thomas frowned. 'Nope. I'll tell you exactly what he said. He said: "My dog has no nose." And Mr. Parker said: "How does he smell?" And that's when Ollie told us that he's stinky.'

Liz resisted the temptation to laugh. She ran her fingers through her son's blond hair. 'It was a joke,' she said. 'A very old one.'

'Then it was a lie, if he hasn't got a dog. And I still shouldn't go to his house, because we don't like liars.' Thomas pulled the grumpiest face he could manage and stomped off to his room.

That evening Liz had to take Thomas to college with her. He fell asleep in the car on the way home, and she struggled to carry him to his bed.

'That was an unsatisfactory arrangement last night, Thomas,' she said during breakfast. Thomas looked up at her with peanut butter on his cheek and nose. 'You're going to have to sort things out with Oliver at school today. Jokes are not lies, you know. They're more like stories.

You would never say Goldilocks and the Three Bears was a fib, would you? It's a story. And a joke isn't a fib either.'

Thomas nodded and spoke through a mouthful of toast. 'A joke isn't a fib. Well, I suppose that's good to know.'

By the end of the day Oliver and Thomas were once more the best of friends, and Thomas was inflicting the dog with no nose joke on everybody he met at school, finishing it on every occasion with the words 'and that's not a fib, it's a joke, so you can laugh'.

A week or so later he and his mother were walking their usual route to school when Thomas stopped and pointed to a high wooden gate. There was a small enamelled notice screwed to it. 'That says something about a dog,' said Thomas.

'Well done,' said Liz. 'Now can you tell me what it says about the dog?'

Thomas stared for a moment. 'No,' he said. 'The first word's too big and hard.'

'Beware,' said his mother. 'It says "beware of the dog".'

Thomas's whole body went rigid. 'No,' he said. 'I can't go past that gate. We have to go back. We have to.'

'Why?' His mother grabbed his arm as he turned to run towards home. 'Don't be a silly boy. Come along. We'll be late to school. You don't want a late mark, do you?'

Thomas adopted his stubborn face, crossed his arms and stood with his knees straight and legs apart. 'We're not going past a dangerous dog,' he announced. 'You don't want me to be bitten, do you?'

'Thomas, we've passed that notice on Mr. Wilson's gate every day since you started school and you've never been bitten. I don't believe he even has a dog. I've never seen one. Have you?'

Thomas looked thoughtful. 'No, I haven't. But he must have got one. So we can't go past.'

Liz sighed. 'Yes we can, Thomas. I expect it's just a sign Mr. Wilson put up on his gate years ago to stop burglars coming in. He's pretending to have a dog to scare them away. Now come along.'

Thomas relaxed a little. 'All right,' he said. 'But you must hold my hand, just in case.'

They hurried on to school without further incident. On the return trip that evening Thomas tugged at his mother's sleeve. 'Mum, Mr. Wilson's not a nice man.'

'Really darling? What makes you say that?'

'He tells fibs. My teacher says "beware of the dog" isn't a joke or a story, it's a warning. But if you warn somebody about something and it isn't really there, then you're telling a lie, aren't you?'

'I suppose so, sweetheart. But it's only a little white lie.'

Thomas was almost home when he announced that you couldn't see a joke, so it couldn't possibly be white.

When Thomas's father arrived on Friday night to take Thomas for the weekend, he looked somewhat worse for wear. 'Have you been drinking?' Liz asked. 'You know the rules. No booze when you have Thomas.' She sniffed the air in front of his face. 'You have, haven't you?'

'I was out last night, but none since. Honest.'

'Liar. I can smell it. Thomas stays here.'

Thomas stood behind her leg as though trying to hide.

'Only one. Hair of the dog and all that.'

Thomas screamed. Tears started. 'What dog? You can't have dog hair without a dog. What dog, Daddy? Mummy, I'm never going to Daddy's again. Not if he's got a dog.'

Liz sighed and gave her ex-husband a sharp look. 'Now you've done it,' she said. 'Explain that one to him, if you can.' She turned to face her son. 'Don't worry. He hasn't got a dog. But as far as I'm concerned, you're not going anyway. You can stay home with me this weekend. Daddy's in the doghouse.'

F H LEE

still so easy to shut down shut off keep away for today blame those who can
before buried now by centuries of depth I never knew existed but I can stand
their feet hover above them and spew like an untamed shrew about you and the
and us and how could I and how much mist falls and fails to forgive and love mo
then dig even deeper and creep along each ditch until the gasping for breath hur
my heart and head and hands are swollen but blue skin shreds as still mo
shrapnel sinks deeper into bone since optimism would force me to remove it bit
bit surgically still insanely hopeful that I might turn a corner and have no mo
to complain about since it cannot possibly get easier and we are away to the rac
onward and upward but are held at the throat by ghosts who did more suffer
more put up with more never dared cave kept it meshed up inside like a hern
not able to exercise opinion or expose glints of blue sky but remain chained inta
with heads tilted forward like the noble bullrush on October stalks bravi
November winds awaiting December snows to coat them and create silent shelt
for invisible contemplation where softened skin seeds and feeds new fur and v
somehow pretend it never happened at all
but it did
and it will
and I won't
ever stop
trying to fight my way through each day for the one place I know is worth going
as we stare at a clear but far North star, try to touch near warmth within
make sweet love last, near or far
make time to stare, fill tonight with nexts
consider how far is near, as beginnings wait, nows end
harder now than ever
to reach up
see over
hear out
defend
blend

GILL TERRY

There were plenty of spare seats on the morning train but he chose instead to stand in the space between two carriages. He watched through the window as the flat Cheshire plains rolled by. The wind-driven rain smeared itself across the grimy glass like so many tears shed in silence.

It had come to this. He'd had his chance to start anew and he'd cocked it up spectacularly.

His RAF uniform was immaculate. He'd Brasso'd the five metal buttons on his jacket and polished his shoes until they shone like mirrors. His propeller flashes, one on each arm, had been added only weeks before when he'd finished his basic training. God, what he'd gone through for that! And now it was all thrown away, all ruined. By the end of this afternoon his career would be over. His life would be over. He'd already planned it. That's why there was a handgun in his kitbag.

*

John Smith. A plain name and perfect for a boy who tried hard not to stand out, to stay under the radar. Not that it completely protected him from the bullying. At school he was no academic. While his younger sister Ruth got top grades without even trying he struggled with every subject. If he could have made up for it by prowess in sports it might have helped, but he was small for his age, had poor hand to eye co-ordination and no stamina, and when his class filed into the changing rooms his name was always the last to be chosen when making up teams. He was the one the other boys picked on. They threw his clothes around as he shivered in the showers, called him Pimple.

"Hey, Pimple! How did you get to be so thick?"

"Pimple! Why are your trousers wet? Have you pissed yourself?"

"Look everyone! Pimple's crying again!"

It was no better at home. His father Rolf was not a well man. Not well in the head, that is. An illness that nobody ever spoke of. Ruth could wrap her father round her little finger, but however hard John tried he could never do anything right. Life for him was a catalogue of humiliations, and nobody intervened. Until one evening, late in summer when John was fifteen, that is. If, in the aftermath, no-one could recall what it was that had finally made John snap, the incident itself remained vivid in the minds of every member of that household.

For many years a pair of Japanese naval swords had hung on the living room wall, a souvenir from some wartime escapade long ago. Now one of them was in John's hands, the scabbard removed, the razor-sharp tip up against Rolf's Adam's apple, pinning him against the wall.

It was John's grandmother who talked him down that day. Later she held him to her breast and let him sob until he was done, then made him hot milk with a little brandy and put him to bed. She sat beside him until he fell asleep and left the bedside light on until the morning. The swords were given away that same night, replaced on the wall by a framed picture of a bluebell wood. Nobody referred to it.

Not long afterwards John's mother disappeared leaving the children behind. Rolf shut himself in his study with the curtains drawn and seldom came out. Ruth went to stay with her grandmother but John, sixteen now and about to leave school, was left to fend for himself at home with his ailing, unpredictable father.

One afternoon soon afterwards John took a bus to Liverpool and walked into the RAF Recruiting Office. It is some measure of how desolate John's life had become that this puny, diffident boy was eager to trade it for life on the parade ground and in the gym, and with all the other hardships that basic training would throw at him. He signed up on the spot for 25 years.

Was it the discipline, the routine, the loss of his hated nickname that produced the transformation, or had John just needed to leave behind his dysfunctional home life in order to blossom? Whatever the explanation, he didn't just tear out a page from his old life – he threw away the whole book and began afresh.

In the New Recruit's Club he became a passable poker player. His mates called him Pip, short for pip-squeak - so much more acceptable than Pimple. They prized his small stature since he was able to squeeze through tiny windows to let the bigger blokes into the women's quarters, and fit through small gaps in the perimeter fence to do the odd bit of pilfering. More than the odd bit, to be truthful.

When he came home on leave after his basic training he felt invincible. He wore his uniform with pride. In his local pub the landlord served him on the house, even though he was still under age. Travelling in uniform was a cinch, too - folk always stopped for a man in uniform trying to hitch a lift.

He'd been back on base for less than 24 hours when his Sergeant bawled his name.

'Smith J.P., what trouble did you get into on your weekend leave?'

'None, Sir!'

'Then why does the Flight Lieutenant want to see you?'

'Don't know, Sir!'

'Get yourself smartened up and Corporal Mathers will take you over.'

When he was marched into the Flight Lieutenant's office he saw there was a second officer in the room: an RAF Police Sergeant, immediately identifiable by the red MP badge on his sleeve.

'Smith, Sergeant Groves from the RAF Police is present to hear your answers to the questions I'm about to ask. Think very carefully before you reply. Were you on leave the weekend just passed?'

'Yes Sir!'

'On your return journey to this base did you accept a lift from a member of the public?'

There was a moment's pause before John answered.

'Yes Sir!'

'Smith, did you steal anything from that person's car?'

'No Sir!'

'I see. There has been a complaint from a member of the public. He says that he gave a lift to a man wearing an RAF uniform, and that later he discovered that his wife's handbag was missing from the back seat of the car. Think carefully before you answer. Do you know anything at all about the whereabouts of that handbag?'

'No Sir!'

'Then you have nothing to worry about. Sergeant Groves will be liaising with the civilian Police to investigate this matter. It is possible you may be charged and if so you will need to appear at a Magistrates Court. I must tell you, Smith that if you are found guilty this will go on your service record. Your career with the RAF will be adversely affected, the chances of promotion up the ranks effectively over. Do you understand?

'Yes Sir.'

*

Now that day had come. The train rattled over the points as it approached the station, and John considered his options.

He remembered Mr Meadows, the old fellow who had stopped to pick him up. He'd said he was one of the last men to be called up for National Service, and had done a year at Warton aerodrome in 1957. He was 74 now, two generations older than John, but they'd chatted like comrades. They'd compared notes about their basic training and John guessed he must have told him then where he was currently based. But even if he hadn't it would have been simple for the Police to check. There couldn't be many RAF servicemen recently Passed Out, returning to a base in North West England on that same day. But that didn't make him guilty, did it? The court could agree that an elderly couple had got themselves confused. He would plead Not Guilty and hope for the best.

But then there were the photographs. Snapshots of someone's family. One of an old man in a deckchair, some little girls in white dresses, and the one he liked the best: a large lady in a pinny, beaming at the camera, her hands kneading bread on a floury kitchen table. Just like his Grandma. He'd pocketed the cash and got rid of the handbag long before he got back to base, but he couldn't chuck out the photos that he'd found inside – they'd be special to someone.

If he made a clean breast of it he could hand back the photographs, but if he did that his RAF career was gone, and with it all that was meaningful in his life. He couldn't contemplate coming back home with his tail between his legs to face his father's ridicule and condemnation. He'd rather die.

The train pulled in to Liverpool Lime Street. John had plenty of time. He deposited his kit bag in Left Luggage then went into the newsagents on the station forecourt and bought a small pad of paper and a packet of envelopes. In the station café he sat with a mug of tea and began to write.

'Dear Mr and Mrs Meadows. I am very sorry for what I've done. I can't return your money but I wanted to give you these. Yours sincerely. LAC Smith, J.P.'

He tried to write more letters: one for his sister, another for his grandmother. He got as far as writing 'Dear Ruthie' on one, but then had to give up. He'd try again afterwards.

He was crossing the street to reach the Magistrates Court when he saw an old man in a trilby just ahead of him, leaning on a walking stick and slowly climbing the stone steps that led to the heavy glass door. It was Mr Meadows.

It's now or never, Pip, John said to himself.

He ran up the steps two at a time and held open the door for Mr Meadows as he approached.

'Thanks, Son,' said the old man, before he realised who it was.

'I need to give you this,' said John, and thrust the envelope into Mr Meadows' hand before he turned away.

It was 45 minutes later when John's case was called. The usher led him into the dock at the back of the courtroom where he remained standing, his back straight and his hands by his sides, as the judges filed in. The prosecutor rose to his feet and addressed the court.

'Your Worships, as a result of new information recently come to hand, the prosecution will offer no evidence, and asks for the case to be dismissed.'

As John left the courtroom he spotted Mr Meadows up in the public gallery. The old man stood, put on his hat, and brought his right hand up to his brow to give John a smart salute.

EFFIE MERRYL

I'd always planned to take refuge in the lavatory. My initial delight when I realised she'd chosen a first-class carriage waned rapidly with the reality of having to wait inside the tiny disgusting box. The stench of slopped urine and railway-issue soap clogged up my nose as I chugged this way and that, my body weaving against the beast manoeuvring the tracks.

I thought of her sitting out there in the carriage, her head lolling to one side. I imagined her tongue hanging out, a red slab of raw meat on the verge of turning purple, her eyes popping and bulging like a bull-frog. I watched my hands squeeze her throat, tight, tight, a little tighter. And snap.

I opened my eyes as I felt my heart thump hard in my chest. I was finally close enough to do this. I'd waited long, so very long. Nine years is such a long time.

****

Tick-Tock. Tick-Tock. The huge clock on the wall behind the dock tick-tocks. I hear the imaginary clicks of the thin black hands as the battery-operated clock tick-tocks. Can anyone else hear it? Tick. Tock. Tick. Tock.

The foreman stands, the elected member of the twelve, a balding man, a nervous, frightened man. A respectable man one would presume. Somebody's husband. Somebody's dad. A granddad. Perhaps.

Every face turns to look at him. Many pairs of eyes stare black, beads of anticipation unrelenting as the clock tick-tocks. The judge, the barristers, the clerks, the press, the police, the public gallery. Me. The defendant. Every eye upon me. No lashes flick. No eye blind.

The foreman turns the small rectangle of white paper in his hand with nervous fingers and gives an almost imperceptible twitch, a slight shake he doesn't want anyone to see. He folds it, opens it, creases it and looks down.

I know he already knows what it says when he looks at the judge, searching for his eye, his acknowledgment, some understanding. He does not look at me. He doesn't look anywhere near the dock. It is then that I know.

Tick. Tock.

Guilty.

I am guilty. Convicted of indecent assaults, my hands on many boys. And of perverting the course of justice.

I turn and look at her. I see my snarl rather than feel it as my upper lip peels back. I show her the fleshy bits, the bright red lumpy bumps rich with blood pounding through my veins so hot I think they are going to burst open, blood red spouting across the court room. Of course, they don't explode so I expose my teeth, dull sock-grey and little, like they belong to a teenage anorexic.

I pretend to snarl. Or maybe I actually do. I remind myself of a dog my uncle once kept. A bit thin, a bit scabby, a bit rabid, a bit mad. I raise my arm and point at her.

'You,' I whisper.

She shifts her bottom along the wooden bench as my finger remains pointing at her. I spy the thin wedge of black beneath my nail. In that instant we are the only two people in the courtroom and the world stops tick-tocking and my life stands in the silence between us.

The judge, the barristers, the clerks, they all ignore me like I don't exist. Like I am a court jester they don't want to notice. An elephant taking up too much room. They do nothing but talk like I am not there.

They are used to such actions, such reactions, especially from bitter convicts angry at perceived injustice. Angry especially towards the police. Especially towards a woman.

The jury members, twelve good people and true, all raise their eyebrows at the shot of drama. Mellow drama. I stay in the dock. I point my dirt-crusted finger. I snarl. It's nothing. I'm impotent really. They look but don't want to yet can't control themselves. So I laugh. Ha. Haha. Hahaha. It is so funny.

I see them look at me but they don't linger because they are the ones who have condemned me to an indeterminable sentence. They don't want that dirty-horned nail that looks like it belongs to Satan pointing anywhere at them so they look at her, her, that detective with the grim face and podgy ankles.

I see two of them slyly flick an eye in my direction, pretending not to watch. I imagine myself as Hannibal Lector as I slurp my tongue and grin at them. My barrister makes his case, my case, for leniency as I protest my innocence again, instructing my barrister to lodge an appeal.

He ignores me as he continues his monologue in monotone. It's black and white words, up and down like a boring piano chord. He misses off the bit about my previous good character because I don't have one. It's a tell-tale sign for the jury, should they know to look out for it, and maybe some did, maybe some didn't when they did their condemning.

The jury listens as the barrister for the prosecution reveals my dirty secrets. A young woman on the back bench cries, sobbing into a lace handkerchief, her with a perfect life that has vanilla candles in the bathroom as she soaks her aching back. Vanilla candles in her lonely bedroom too. A middle-aged man hangs his head. Perhaps he's guilty too? Several look away. Others just stare ahead. Nobody speaks as the judge addresses me, the guilty defendant.

The Lord Justice Hootenanny doesn't linger over words as he sentences me. Fifteen years imprisonment. No deliberation. No pause. Straight to jail.

It matters not. I won't do fifteen. Might not even do five. I know what to do, how to play the game. How to bide my time. I'll get fit. Get fatter. Get my teeth fixed. And clean my nails. I'll be a good boy for the judge. A reformed man.

The jury are dismissed. They file out into the safety of a warm room laden with fresh espresso coffee and curled up sandwiches. They are excused from further service at the court and they will take with relish and relief the expenses form handed out to thank them for conducting their civic duty.

As I'm taken down from the dock and led through the open back door of the courtroom in handcuffs, I cast a backward glance just before the door clangs shut. Her eye catches mine and the deal is done, whether she wants it or knows it. It could take a long time but that's something I have a lot of. Time.

Tick. Tock.

***

A seven year stretch. They release me. Like an itch, I was scratched and it was time to move on. Like a spring, they expect me to bounce back. Only I reckon the elastic might snap this time.

I'd been a good boy, done everything they asked. The counselling sessions talking to some pretty girl shrink who teased us with her stocking tops – only she was fat and ugly and the only stocking should have been over her head. I had to pretend she was a pretty one though, just to get through the rubbish I was expected to spout. I did the kitchen duties and the gutsy jobs nobody else wanted. I did things for the screws and in turn, they did things for me. Like turning the other way when I needed them to. That sort of thing. Play the game, poker-face.

Like all sex offenders I was subject to conditions. Silly thing but when they locked me up I didn't know how to use the internet or computer so there were no specific terms in my order. I learned a lot inside. About search engines. Cookies. And Internet footprints. Canny, eh?

When I got out, Probation found me a flat in Leeds. I didn't care where it was. Anywhere would do. With a computer the world was open and free and fresh and mine.

It didn't take me long to find her. Social networking. The more people do it, they less they can resist it. Until finally - Google becomes their name.

It took less than six months for me to find out which street she lived in, where she went on holiday, the names of her children, and what colour underwear she wore last Sunday. It was that easy. Twitter. Facebook. LinkedIn ...

Last Thursday I was watching Question Time with one eye on Twitter. I saw it quick, before it disappeared down the plughole of tweets. She would be in Paddington train station on Saturday. It was a book day and she was meeting other bibliophiles. She would be on her own. Her and a suitcase and nobody else.

She was then going all the way home to Abergavenny to some remote cottage she'd moved into with her family to escape the hub-bub of her previous life. What she hadn't realised was a small place is no place to hide and everyone knows your name. And what they don't know, they make up. I could have told her that, had she wanted to listen. And you cannot tear a single page from your life, not with the internet.

There was only one train going from London to Abergavenny on Saturday afternoon. It went every afternoon at three o'clock. I prepared well, packed my rucksack like I was going climbing – change of clothing, rope, knife, flask, bandages, bin-bags. Gun. Tick!

My phone was charged. My body eager. My soul willing. I followed her every tweet without her even knowing of my existence. I'd been on her for months and she didn't even know. I never tweeted her but had she come across me she would see I'd invented an online persona of my own. Male/female/ambiguous. I sent random tweets to celebrities who never replied and a few random folk who did. Nothing suspicious, nothing to raise concern, a casual follower she didn't know existed.

I sat with a coffee outside the burger bar in the train station. She wouldn't recognise me. Not now. Not all these years on. Not with my red wig hair, dark glasses, teeth fixed, and body beefed up. It had been such a very long time. I'd be right out of context and far away from her zone. She never expected me to be part of her life again. I'd given her false security. I doubt she even remembered my name.

I spotted her instantly. She was trailing a little black suitcase down the ramp from one of the other platforms. She propped the case against the counter of a posh coffee stall and she ordered something fancy, just as she would. She took a seat and I saw her manipulating the screen of her smart phone. I reached for my mobile, head down, the right numbers. Bingo!

Twitter. Every time, Twitter. She was chatting in full view to a someone who wrote proper books the like of which she could only fantasise about. I followed their conversation. This writer, a popular children's author, was on her train too but was going to Oxford. And in her carriage, M. For First Class. M for mine, all mine, for me. She told the writer her seat was 55A. She, the sycophant, told the author she'd read her work to her lovely boys. I remember reading them to my lovely boys, back when I had them and before she had taken them away from me, made them tell terrible lies. I'd only ever loved them. All of them. She would never understand that.

I finished my bitter coffee. Precision. By the time her train was ready to pull in I was waiting a few feet away. She wouldn't notice me. She was too busy looking out for her pseudo-famous pal to see me loitering. I watched her, fat ankles and all, as she climbed aboard, waving frantically with a fish-mouth smile on her fat face.

I smiled. Oh yes, she was happy now. And so was I.

I kept my rucksack clasped tight to my belly. I wasn't leaving it on any old luggage shelf to be picked up by a stranger. It was mine, all mine. Just like she would be very soon.

The carriage smelt of warm bodies and sour freebie gin given to first-class customers only. There were more people than I imagined travelling first-class. I pretended to look for my seat, clocking the destinations on the tickets. Most would be leaving well before Abergavenny. I found a vacant pew. It might as well have had my name on it. In the meantime, I'd wait in the lavatory. Locked in and dreaming of her fat red tongue lolling down, thick and lush. But that's a sexual motivated crime and it will never do. As much as I'd love to take the hands on approach and squeeze the life from her, squash out her last breath, I know how it must be done.

On a mid-autumn day like this it will be dark at the right time and before she alights there will be but me and her in the carriage, waiting for her departure.

***

She's dead. Shot in the head. Quiet. Clean. A revenge killing. These days I make sure I don't let my fingernails get dirty. I walk down the train through almost empty carriages, all the way to G. Or F. Or maybe D? Somewhere where the second class people sit, where they slumber, read, and get drunk. When the train stops, I alight and disappear into the night somewhere remote but not caring where. Job done.

YUE YUE

JEFF PINKNEY

It takes the cries of a worthless girl to awaken the world,
there is something wrong with us and it's my fault,
we'd pray, but the temple was replaced by merchant stalls,
-the homeless gods are wailing from the ether,
while the Bureau tries to wash the blood away.

Forgive us YueYue, we watched and then walked by,
and now your pain holds us hostage for remorse.
Live, to find compassion not iniquity,
and when I lift my head from shame, may I not be,
so callously deserving of a worthless world.

for Wang Yue of Foshan China, 2009-2011

HAZEL

ANNE HAMLETT

I seek inspiration; follow the path
to the river where hazels grow,
a confusion of trunks which arch
into an enchanted world
charged with quicksilver energy.

Curls of smoke strobe sunlight,
carry an echo of brimstone
from charcoal burners deep in woodland.

I reach for nut-laden branches,
gather lustrous russet jewels
amid dark vintage leaves.

It brings memories of hazelnut bread,
and magical stories of tree-spirits
which mother wove in our fragrant
kitchen, waiting for dough to rise.

I rest on mossy stones,
watch speckled salmon feed
on hazelnuts as they drop
into swirls of water.

I sense the spirit of Arianrhod
which spans our two worlds,
with tenuous threads of connection.

A strand of my red hair snags on twigs -
hangs like a votive offering
to appease an ancient deity;
my wish for inspiration
fulfilled.

AN ANGEL TO THE RESCUE

BOB SMITH

Mark slipped into the hospital chapel, not because he was religious but because he knew it would provide a measure of tranquillity, a haven from the persistent intercom voice paging Doctor Whoever. There were only two types of people in the halls - visitors looking lost and bewildered, and staff scurrying as if they were on a matter of life and death. *Which they might be*, Mark admitted. He wanted nothing to do with either variety. *Besides, the chapel might smell of candles and incense, not pine disinfectant and death.* He wasn't religious in any conventional sense, more likely to find something spiritual in an early-morning sunrise than a mosque or synagogue, though lately he had become rather intrigued by the increasing attempts to connect environmentalism and religion. But this visit to the chapel had far more to do with the secular than the sacred.

He had been the only one present when Mr Hyde slipped away, and even that was accidental. He had been at the Forestview Regional Health Centre for an MRI on his shoulder, but as he was taking a short cut through the hospice wing towards the exit, he happened to glance into a room and recognized the distinct moustache. When he had looked into the room from the doorway, he found no one present and that had been entirely depressing. No flowers, no photos, nothing personal at all, just a bed with Mr Hyde in it and a heart monitor chanting an electronic beep. Mr Hyde had been a childhood acquaintance, not a close friend; something like the crystal rock with gold veins he had found when he was ten that he now knew wasn't monetarily valuable but had too many associations to simply discard. He knew Mr Hyde's wife had died long before Mark met him and they hadn't had children. He also knew Mr Hyde was an only child. So he hadn't been shocked at the vacant room, but that didn't make it less sad.

He had entered and quickly realized from the sluggishness of the beeping that Mr Hyde wasn't simply sleeping but in a coma. Over the next several minutes, he realized Mr Hyde's breathing was becoming even slower and shallower as the beeping diminished. When it stopped entirely half an hour later, he realized the monitor could also be watched from the Nurses' Station because someone appeared. When she seemed somewhat taken aback to find him there, he explained his presence. "Sorry," she said, "You aren't family so you can't stay. Unofficially, I'm glad you stopped so he wasn't alone at the end."

"He might not have known I was here," Mark explained.

"We never know what someone in a coma is aware of," she finished.

Mark didn't tell her he had chatted about his childhood memories involving Mr Hyde. *She sounds like she might understand but I still feel slightly foolish*, he thought.

That's why he now needed to find stillness, and the chapel seemed to be the only place that would suffice. Everywhere else in the Healthcare Centre was hectic. He assumed somewhere there were quiet, private offices for administrators and doctors, but he wouldn't be allowed into those retreats. It was either the chapel or the morgue, which he didn't even want to think about.

His eyes were drawn to the stained glass window, the only colourful thing in the spartan room. It featured an angel with a lantern, surrounded by several smaller figures looking at the angel with anticipation or some other hopeful emotion. As he stared, the angel's face was replaced by a vision of Mr Hyde when Mark had first met him.

Mark smiled. Mr Hyde's appearance was about as far from an angel's as a person could find. Even when Mark had first met him twenty years ago, he had unkempt grey eyebrows that looked like one big caterpillar inching across his forehead, a red-veined nose too big for his face, and a bushy moustache which hid his entire upper lip plus a good part of the lower one. Even though Mark had been only seven, many years from the daily razor routine, he had recognized how badly that man on the other park bench needed a shave.

Mark's mother had taken him and his four year-old brother Darryl to the playground as she did most Saturday mornings, and sat Mark on the bench with firm instructions not to leave it while she chased the overactive child, hoping the recreation would exhaust him. It would still be a few years before the school insisted she take Darryl to a paediatrician about his behaviour. The doctor would diagnose it as Attention Deficit Hyperactivity Disorder and prescribe medication to control his impulsive mania. But at the age of seven, all Mark knew was Darryl was a royal pain and their mother usually ignored Mark except for orders and threats she was all too ready to enforce.

She hadn't always been that way. Before Darryl had been born, she was patient and attentive. Now that Mark was a teacher specializing in kids with problems, he understood what had happened. In a child development course he had taken at university, they had spent a few hours learning about the reactions of children when an infant is introduced into the home. He recognized how his mother had done all the right things. She had involved Mark in preparing the nursery. She had let him feel the foetus moving in her belly. She had found photos of Mark as a baby and asked what he remembered and then talked about what he had been like. Above all, she had reassured him a new child would increase the richness of their family, not diminish her love.

But that was before. Darryl was a problem almost from the day he came home. Mark's mother grew more and more haggard, especially after his father left saying he couldn't handle the constant chaos, had to have some peace and quiet. Children usually don't notice things like black lines under a parent's eyes, but Mark did. More significant to him were her temperament changes. An easy-going, loving mother became an angry, impatient one. Minor transgressions which once would have evoked gentle reprimands now brought angry shouting and head-slaps. He almost valued being ignored – almost, but not quite, as he remembered the halcyon days of 'before-Darryl'.

Mark tried to refocus on the angel's glass face, but Mr Hyde's ephemeral one remained superimposed. That reminded him of the reminiscences he had been voicing in Mr Hyde's room.

Mark's mother had directed Mark to the park bench with strict orders not to leave it, orders he knew from painful experience not to ignore. He resentfully watched her chase Darryl towards the set of swings.

A man sat down on the bench across the sandbox but didn't look Mark's way. He unfolded a newspaper and began to read. Out of boredom, Mark made a game of trying to glimpse the man's face whenever he turned a page, without being caught.

Eventually, the man refolded the paper and asked, "So do I pass inspection?" Mark was briefly tempted to run, except for two things - his mother's command and the man's gentle, humorous tone of voice. At school, they had said to be wary of strangers but Mark didn't feel threatened. The man was across the sandbox and made no attempt to stand when he spoke. Besides, he had used a cane as he slowly limped to the bench so Mark was sure he could outrun him if he had to. That didn't help answer the question though, but Mark didn't know what to say so he remained silent.

"What are you doing here by yourself anyway?" the man asked.

Again Mark said nothing, but pointed to his mother trying to slow Darryl's frenzied swinging.

"Why aren't you over there too?"

Mark didn't realize his resentment showed so clearly as he scowled in their direction. The man nodded knowingly. "Brother?" When Mark bobbed his head, he asked, "Why aren't you on the other swing? There's more than one, you know."

Mark didn't like the implication that it was his choice to be left behind so he finally spoke. "Mom told me to stay here." All his resentment came bubbling out. "It takes all her energy to watch Darryl so she does things like this all the time, makes me stay put while he gets to play."

Lines of sympathy appeared in the man's forehead as he nodded again. "Why does she do that?"

Mark still didn't take his eyes off them. "He's hyper so it takes Mom's full attention to keep track of what he's up to. I'm well-behaved so she knows she can trust me." He tried to make it sound like a source of pride.

The man said, "Sounds to me like the one who misbehaves gets rewarded while the responsible one gets punished."

Mark had never put it into those words but that matched his feelings exactly. However, he wasn't about to criticize Mom to a stranger, so he again stayed quiet, not realizing how much his face spoke for him.

"Do you like stories?" the man asked.

Mark nodded. Anything remotely entertaining beat simply sitting on the bench.

"What are your favourite animals?"

A vision of the angry grizzly he had seen on a TV episode of Natural Geographic flashed into Mark's mind at the question. "Bears."

"What a coincidence," the man said. "I happen to know a story that involves three bears, a mother and two cubs, one that was quiet and reliable and one that was constantly doing things without thinking."

When he was an adult, Mark realized it was neither a coincidence that the story involved his favourite animals, nor that the family in it mirrored his own. He didn't remember all the details, but by then they hardly mattered.

Mr Hyde, which was the man's name, had begun to come to the park every Saturday morning around the same time as Mark. He always sat on the bench across, never tried to shift closer like the man who had tried to lure Reggie Blakely from the schoolyard with the promise of a treat.

Mr Hyde always had stories, sometimes about bears but often involving other creatures. When Mark took a Children's Literature course as part of his teacher's training, he recognized many as modified versions of Aesop's Fables. Though he hadn't realized it at the time, many fit particular situations that Mark was currently experiencing, or had lessons about being tolerant and patient. He didn't recognize all the stories though, and was certain Mr Hyde invented those ones.

When he was eight, Mr Hyde told him one about a man whacking a mosquito that was biting him on the nose, thus breaking it. Mr Hyde then said, "Sometimes when we seek revenge, we end up hurting ourselves." Mark had been speculating about hiding Darryl's favourite toys to 'teach him a lesson'. He hadn't stopped to think that Mom might deduce how they had migrated to the garage.

He remembered another incident from the age of nine when he was accusing Darryl of causing some minor problem. "Point at something," Mr Hyde had said. When Mark did, he nodded. "See, there are more fingers in your own direction than the one aimed elsewhere." The following conversation which contrasted self-examination with blaming others was more lesson than discussion, but not a preachy one.

When he was ten, complaining about the exercises the baseball coach made them do, it was a story about a man freeing a struggling butterfly from its cocoon and how that fatally weakened it because effort would have let it build strength.

Now, as an adult, Mark recognized how important Mr Hyde's stories had been. *Without them, I would have remained an angry person, a bitter, blaming, accuser, never satisfied with anything.* At the staff Christmas party last year, Gerald Hudson had said, "I'm sure having a brother like that explains why you have so much patience for the kids you work with." The previous week, Darryl had come to the school, interrupting a staff meeting with a demand that Mark drive him to Walmart, 'right now'. The next day in the staff room before classes started, Mark had had to explain his brother to everyone.

Mark knew that comment from Gerald was completely inaccurate, though he didn't say so. *It wasn't Darryl that made me patient and accepting.* He had long ago realized it was Mr Hyde's stories.

The angel in the window didn't move of course, and Mark found he could dismiss Mr Hyde's features with concentration. He realized sitting in the chapel had worked, that he had shifted from agitation to calm and was almost ready to face other people.

The chapel door opened. *So much for being alone*, Mark thought.

"You stay here," a female voice said. "I'll take Herbie with me to see Grandpa." It was a woman with two boys, one about three who she grasped firmly by the wrist, the other a familiar-looking lad who looked about eight. Mark recognized him from the school playground, a youngster who sullenly watched the other boys playing soccer at recess from a spot beside the fence. He never participated. Mark thought, *I might not have noticed him except for that expression, which usually ranges from morose to surly.*

Then the woman became aware of Mark. "Oops," she said. "This place is usually empty." She looked closer. "Say, you look familiar. Aren't you one of the teachers at Daniel's school?"

When Mark nodded his confirmation, she added, "He won't bother you. He's the quiet one." To Daniel, she said, "I won't be long. Can't be with your brother." Then she left, dragging Herbie with her.

Sounds familiar, Mark thought.

To Daniel, he said, "What's your favourite animal?"

He never would have pictured his own features on the angel.

E RUSSELL SMITH

abstracts a fourth dimension
from the landscape. Colours move
the first concerto of October minor
from adagio to rondo,
foolhardy thoughts to fugue, a flight
of resolution into major thirds,
a blue glissando into rose horizon.

The highway passes under us,
turns to gravel, then a trail
with weeds between the tracks.
We are farther from wherever,
closer to ourselves; romantic
or baroque informs a grasp
of paradise before the plough.

Red pizzicato snares our sense
of rustic roadside heritage,
a graphic artist's ploy
to fix our wavering courtesy.
Behind whatever garb, we all
dance naked, whistle love songs
fit for philharmonic company.

BAD RIDDANCE

RACHEL GREEN

I came of age in a time of no heroes.

Privatisation. Pit closures. Picket lines. They'd taken their toll on our family, though my father had always been on the wrong side of the pickets. Not that he was a scab. His father and grandfather had worked the seams but he'd wanted a different life, both for him and the family he'd started prematurely with a quickie round the back of the bowls club. He'd chosen to be a policeman.

It hadn't the stigma it has now. In the seventies a man in uniform was a respected member of the community but the pit closures ended the way of life we'd once enjoyed. The police became the natural enemy of the displaced miners and a housebrick lobbed from the picket line was the natural enemy of my father's skull.

"Where's Da?" I fastened my tie. School was no Easy Street for me, I struggled with most subjects, clever enough to be in the top set from Maths and English, but not so clever as to set myself above me peers – or maybe just clever enough. My father stayed at home now, drawing Invalidity Benefit from people who would likely spit on him in the street. I was accustomed to seeing him in the wood-framed arm chair, watching whatever was on the telly, his drool caught by a towel we kept for the purpose. He knew enough to smile and cry and go to the toilet by himself, but not much else, not more than a few words and phrases to parrot, seemingly at random.

He used to be a burly man, six-foot two and about as wide. I thought he was a giant when I was little. He used to be able to pick me up with one hand and balance me on his shoulder to see over crowds or the hedges of Hampton Court maze. "Can you see, Jenny? Can you see?" That became one of the things he could remember after the accident, though I'm not sure he ever remembered his daughter. "Can you see, Jenny? Can you see?"

He lost weight when they let him out of hospital. He'd forgotten how to eat and when he was spoon fed, he'd forgotten how to enjoy food. We puréed his favourites into a grey pudding but even bacon didn't tempt him. He pushed everything away and grew steadily stick like until he resembled Bolaji Badejo, the guy who played the monster in Alien. Michael Pembleton, my boyfriend at the time, sneaked into the cinema to see that when we were both underage. They threw him out but let me stay because I looked old enough and he never forgave me for not leaving with him. Da gave me a stern talking to afterwards, though I think it was more about splitting up with Michael than about seeing X-rated films at fourteen.

Even as an idiot Da knew Mum, though. He clung to her like she was his mother rather than his wife and the more weight he lost, the more she was able to pick him up like a great bald baby. (We shaved his head because it stopped him pulling his hair out.). He'd hang off her when they went to the shops, a grown man clinging to the back of a statuesque woman and passers-by would stop and stare open-mouthed at them as she pushed a trolley through the supermarket. After a particularly noisome incident involving a packet of Iced Fancies the manager asked her not to bring him again.

"What?" Mum's voice from the kitchen. More like scourer than dishcloth. "I can't hear you over the kettle, love."

"Where's Da?"

"Is he no' there?" Ma blustered into the living room wringing her hands through a tea towel more hole than thread. Not that she'd ever throw it out. It once belonged to her mother and was a link to the past I could neither envisage nor desire. I'd have thrown it out long ago, smelly old thing. A bit like Da, really. I loved him but I can be forgiven for hating him, too.

"He was here a minute ago..." She glanced at the television, a children's puppet show in black and white, and reached to change the channel. "I told him to stop watching rubbish." She raised her voice. "Da? Are you in the toilet? Davy?"

When there was no reply I checked. I knew he wasn't upstairs because I'd just come down but we had an outside lavvy as well. How she thought he could be there I don't know, because he'd have had to go past her in the kitchen. While I was outside I checked the greenhouse and the garden shed, surprised it was so empty. Da liked to collect things in his shed. Buckets, plastic bags, soft toys, broken dolls. Anything that attracted his attention was grabbed and stuffed inside his shirt for later inspection. It drove mum up the wall but she let him fill the shed with his treasures. I returned to the kitchen. "He's not outside."

"He must be somewhere."

Thanks, Mum, for stating the obvious. "He's not here, is he? Has he gone out the front?"

Mum bustled through the living room to the tiny front hall and opened the door. No sign of Da, but his shoes were missing from the rack and the empty dustbin was in the street, the dustcart two hundred yards past. "Davy?" Her piercing shriek was loud enough to wake the dead to begin with but she upped it a notch anyway. "Davy!"

Neighbours began appearing on the street. What's up, Glad? Where's your Davy?

"He's gone missing." Mum stood in the middle of the road looking first one way, then the other. We were lucky it wasn't the main street. There was precious little traffic down our road. "Davy?" There was no reply but the rumble of the bin lorry in the distance and the clatter of bins as the dustmen emptied to bins.

"What happened to all his stuff?"

"What stuff?" She stared at the dust lorry, her brow beetling as she watched the men work.

"His stuff. His treasures." I pulled on her arm to get her attention. "The shed's empty."

"Oh, that." The neighbours were beginning to congregate around us so she lowered her voice. "I got rid of them yesterday."

Thursdays were the days he went to the psychiatric clinic to give Mum a respite day. They thought it was enough but we knew it wasn't. Not that we could do anything about it. The Widows and Pensioners Fund paid for his care on Thursdays but there was no way we could afford another. It was enough of a palaver to get him there and back.

"You can't. You know what he's like."

The whole street knew what he was like when he misplaced one of his treasures. Imagine a two-year old having a tantrum and then imagine a six foot man in its place.

She didn't answer me. She just started running toward the distant lorry and the clanking of dustbins. An athlete she wasn't but imagine a snowball rolling down a mountain gathering size and momentum and that was my mum going down the street with the pace and disposition of a rhinoceros who'd just been told his nose would make an aphrodisiac. She shouted in that high-pitched, loud-hailer voice again. "Stahp! Davy!"

She was right on the button. Da's head popped up at the back of the lorry like a bald jack-in-the-box on an extra-strong spring, just as one of the bin men was about to press the button to compress all the rubbish. He turned when he heard the shout and I didn't blame him for looking afraid when he caught sight of Mum barrelling down the road like a juggernaut without brakes. A moment later and Da would have been squished like a toothpaste tube under the pneumatic pistons. The man shouted to the driver and the truck shuddered to a halt, the other bin men putting down their burdens to see what was causing the commotion.

Da had ducked down again by the time Ma arrived, barely out of breath. She was like one of those people you read about in the papers, able to pick up a car with one hand in order to save a child, except that Da was no child but a man as old as she with a wiry strength equal to that of the riddling creature from The Hobbit. I thought for a moment he was hiding from Mum's wrath but he reappeared a moment later with a doll I recognised from the shed, one with a chipped black face and eyes painted open. He held it triumphantly in the air.

"What are you doing there?" The man who a moment before had been about to crush Da now shouted at him in anger. "You could have been killed you stupid great tit."

Da's glee at the recovery of his doll faded, his smile twisting into a wail of grief and fear. Mum, of course, rounded on the man, one meaty fist pressed to her hip and the pointing at him like a belligerent policeman's truncheon. "What did you have to go and shout at him for? Now you've upset him."

"He could have been killed..."

"But he wasn't, was he? Do you know how difficult it is to make him happy again?"

By this time the rest of the neighbours had caught up, some of them, unused to such exercise on a Friday morning, puffing with the effort. I hurried to Mum's side, worried for Da but pleased to be missing double-maths at school. "It's your fault. You took his treasures away."

"I just empty the bins, love." He tried to defend himself but it was too late. The gathering crowd had sympathy for my father. They may have disliked or even hated him as a professional but against outsiders – and people who didn't live on our street were all outsiders – they closed ranks. Shouts and jeers buffeted him from all sides.

Mum went to the back of the wagon to rescue Da. Those trucks stink but even her fastidious cleaning habits and aversion to germs were no match for her determination to retrieve her husband. He was still crying even as he clambered up her, clutching the doll in one thin-fingered grip.

"The poor love." Margery Morris reached into the truck, barely hesitating before she pulled out an old sock and folded her hand inside it. Rather her than me, I thought. No telling where it had been, but a moment later it was a living, breathing rabbit, or possibly a sheep. Da reached for it, clutching it to his chest with the doll.

Mrs. Wilcox from number fifty-six offered him a cabbage from her vegetable bin as if the green-veined vegetable would dry his tears. Mr Davis, remembering Da's penchant for post boxes and fire engines, offered tea in a bright red pot filched from the bin at number seventy-one, while Mrs Simcox (whose husband often cut our lawn in exchange for a slice of Mum's fruit cake) offered a large jug of fresh milk from the goat they kept in the back garden. Mum took it on his behalf.

The neighbourhood men surged forward en masse like a motorcycle gang sans their two-wheeled agents of destruction. They were a rag-tag band dressed in salvaged clothes, their hair unkempt and awry, beards either wispy and dangling or thick as compost, each one holding aloft some token of esteem, a memento of their companionship with Da. A football pennant for a club long dismissed from the premier league; a flag from a foreign country they'd once fought together, a plastic trophy from a fairground rifle range. He dismissed them all, batting them away with his hands, the roseate veins popping across his cheeks as he howled his despair.

Lizzie Beckwith (whose husband Da could never stand) stepped forward holding a live rat by the tip of its tail. What good that was supposed to do I don't know but Da reached for it, his bare toes digging into the soft folds of Mum's flesh as he shifted his weight. The milk jug went flying from her hand to spill upon the soft earth but his tears dried as he closed his pale, meaty fist over the rodent. His wailing faded and he dropped both doll and sock to cradle the vicious little brute to his cheek. It didn't bite.

With Da quiet at last, Mum turned and, like a galleon in full sail, marched calmly back down the street. The neighbours followed in twos and threes, the street slowly emptying. I turned back to the flabbergasted bin man. "Thanks."

"No worries, love." He bent to pick up the doll and the sock, the milk jug and the cabbage and looked at me, his eyebrows raised. I nodded and into the truck they went. We'd have to get a cage for the rat but if it cured him of collecting treasures, I'd get used to it. The truck started up again as I turned away.

I might have grown up in a time of no heroes, but I grew up in a time where community mattered more than social networking, and a small kindness was worth the smile of a once-proud man.

SPARROW

COLIN RENNIE

Adrienne,
your words are like sparrows
disappearing from gardens,
town centres,
and city parks.
They are missed.
You leave crumbs
for us to pick on
as we scramble around.
Late last night
I heard a bird singing,
breast puffed up,
throat ringing,
velvet like your voice.
A poor lost bird,
blown off course,
alone in the pitch dark.

THE WRACK LINE

MANDY PANNETT

Shoreline of creatures on the edge:
cormorant, lugworm, crab.
A sparse and liminal frontier, refuge
for desperate men.

You are restless and distracted –
shushing me to silence as if
listening for things. You check your phone again, again,
scuff up the shingle with your foot,
make a shape of boat.

In darkening light
an ocean may heave its cargo over and down.
You shiver and wait, noticing
how seaweed along the wrack line
drowns in bubbles of foam.

CONTRIBUTORS:

By day, **Vicky Daddo**, from Gippsland, Australia, writes jargon for local government. At night, to redress the balance, she writes short fiction. She has been published in Woman's Day, That's Life Fast Fiction, Award Winning Australian Writing 2009 and 2013, 100 Stories for Queensland and other anthologies. She has won or been shortlisted for many local, national and international competitions.

Rachel Green is a forty-something writer from Derbyshire, England. She lives with her two partners and three dogs. Her novel 'An Ungodly Child' paved the way for a succession of novels in the mythic town of Laverstone. She also writes poetry, paints and illustrates. When not writing, Rachel walks her dogs, potters in the garden, drinks copious amounts of tea and practises Brazilian jiu jitsu. She twitters a haiku daily. www.leatherdyke.co.uk is a portal site to her books and blogs. She can also be found on Facebook (Rachel Green) and Twitter (@leatherdykeuk)

Anne Hamlett: Writer/ sculptor/ artist /teacher. She recently studied with York University to gain a Creative Writing Diploma. Main love is poetry and currently working towards a collection of poems for publication. Over the last few years she's had poems accepted and published in various anthologies and work included on local radio programmes.

Francis Hayes worked as a lawyer in local government until he was offered the opportunity to retire at the age of fifty to help his employer save money. When not writing he makes enamel jewellery and ornaments that he sells at craft fairs in North and West Yorkshire.

Born in 1946, **Joss Hayes** has been writing almost ever since. Although she prefers to write short stories and the occasional novella and does not regard herself as a poet, she can still recite a poem she had published in Elizabethan Magazine in about 1956.

F.H.Lee writes from Oxford County, Ontario, Canada. After 20+ years in cities (YYZ/YYC), Francine returned to her small-town Ontario roots, where nature is embraced as kin, to raise four children (now teens). Local & international poetry contest wins appear in anthologies, and her poems/short fiction/non-fiction span 30 odd years in traditional print or online formats.

Effie Merryl lives in the land of the Scots. When Effie isn't hard at work being a wife, mother and a businesswoman she spends her time writing fiction, faction, reading more, and browsing the net.

Mandy Pannett works freelance in the UK as a creative writing tutor, editor and adjudicator of poetry competitions. She is the author of four poetry collections and a novella. A pamphlet of new work is due to be published in 2014 by Pighog Press.

In addition to writing poems and short stories, **Rhonda Parrish** is the publisher of Niteblade Magazine, enjoys editing anthologies for other publishers and maintains a website at http://www.rhondaparrish.com

Jeff Pinkney has had poems published by Tridentine, All Rights Reserved Literary Journal, and Lucid Forge (National University Poetry Contest). His poetry has been featured in concert productions, Dressed in Love and The Poet and the Singer. Jeff's debut novel for children is set for release by Orca Book Publishers, in fall of 2014.

Douglas Pugh lives in the Haliburton Highlands, ON where he pretends to be a poet, fiction writer and want-to-be-novelist. He has on rare occasions won prizes for his pretence. He hopes you have a wonderful day.

Colin Rennie is 50 and was born in Aberdeen. Now living in London, plying a trade as a librarian, he has just completed a creative writing course with the Open University.

Bob Smith lives in Central Ontario, Canada, where the summers involve spectacular weather and the winters encourage hibernating. Both inspire writing, whether lounging with a laptop overlooking the lake or hunkered at a desk ignoring the snow. He describes his stories as 'character-driven', rather than 'plot-driven'. People face some kind of challenge and face it with creativity and integrity, often connecting with others as part of the process.

Publishing as **E. Russell Smith**: Canadian, born in Toronto, educated at McGill and Cambridge, many years a teacher in Ottawa, now commuting between Ottawa and Hollywood CA, when not travelling to remote parts of the world. Writer for hire, journalist, novelist and recently a full-time poet.

Gill Terry lives on a Scottish island. She enjoys writing poetry and short fiction. Examples of her work can be found in anthologies published in by TheRightEyedDeer Press (*Body Parts and Coal Dust*; *Club Eclectic: The Stirred Poet*; *To the edge of there and back*), and by The Skye Reading Room (*Words from an Island*).

Eilidh Thomas writes poetry and short stories, some of which have been published in print and online. She lives in the north of Scotland with her husband and her dog.

www.ingramcontent.com/pod-product-compliance
Lightning Source LLC
Chambersburg PA
CBHW021130130626
46554CB00002B/950